HER STAND-IN FAKE FIANCÉ

AN OLDER BROTHER'S BEST FRIEND'S ROMANCE

CINDY ROLAND ANDERSON

WINSOME
PRESS
PUBLISHING

Cover Design: Valerie Bybee Photography

Editor: Valerie Bybee Editing

For Cami, Christina, Christine, Jennifer, Kim, Kimberely, Sarah, Rachelle and Tayrn. Thank you for your friendship, love, and support. You are the best, and I love you all so much!

HER STAND-IN FAKE FIANCÉ

She secretly has a crush on him.

He knows she's off-limits.

What happens if they break all the rules?

When someone posts a picture of Presley trying on a diamond ring with a mystery man, the whole world assumes she's getting married. Instead of setting the record straight, her publicist decides this is the perfect launch for her career and confirms the engagement.

Under pressure from the network to reveal her fiancé on national TV, her older brother's best friend volunteers to fill the role. Only, it's not a fake relationship for Presley. She's loved Kade for years.

He's just doing her a favor…

At least that's what she thinks...

Until they kiss under the mistletoe.

CHAPTER 1

PRESLEY

The Princess Warrior is getting married, but who is her Prince Charming?

Presley Windsor stared at her phone and read the words over again, hoping this was a joke. She wasn't engaged. Heck, she didn't even have a boyfriend right now. Guys were too big of a distraction.

Sucking in a quick breath, she took a screenshot and then navigated to her contacts. Tapping on her new PR agent's name, she hoped the social media queen knew how to fix this. The phone immediately rolled over to voicemail, meaning Zuri was probably still asleep and had her phone off. Her new agent was twenty-five, just two years older than Presley, and Zuri's day didn't typically start until after ten in the morning. Presley didn't have the luxury to sleep in, not that she could anyway. She'd always been a morning person. Not sure what else to do, she decided to leave a voicemail and would follow up with a text.

"Hey, Zuri." Presley realized her mistake as soon as she heard the sound that activated her phone's built-in intelligent assistant.

"I'm listening," her phone said in a male Australian voice. Once Presley had asked her phone if she could change Siri's name to Chris Hemsworth. Her phone had responded that changing names would be very confusing. Clearly, her phone was the one confused because Zuri and Siri were not even close as far as Presley was concerned.

"I'm not talking to you," Presley said irritably.

"Who are you talking to then?" Travis asked, coming into the kitchen from the garage. He dropped his duffle bag to the floor and untucked his firefighter shirt. Although a little bleary-eyed, he looked pretty good after coming off a forty-eight-hour shift.

"No one," Presley answered at the same time her phone asked for clarification. Giving up on leaving a message, she ended the call and turned to her brother.

"I'm engaged."

"Come again?" Travis asked, his blue eyes widening in shock.

Presley quickly opened her photos to find the last screenshot and held up her phone. "According to Twitter, the Princess Warrior is engaged."

Travis grabbed the phone from her and scanned the screen. "Is this a joke?" he asked, handing her cell back.

"It's not a very funny one," Presley said, typing in her name to do a quick search online. She gasped when the top results showed a picture of her trying on an engagement ring along with basically the same caption as the Tweet.

"Just great." Presley tapped on the screen and showed her brother. "Someone got a picture of us picking out Brynlee's ring and decided to draw their own conclusions." She'd gone ring shopping with her brother a few nights ago. The photo clearly identified Presley. Travis was wearing a ball cap and had his head bent, so his face wasn't visible.

Travis started laughing. "What are your fans going to do when they find out Prince Charming is your brother?"

"Ha ha." Presley opened Instagram and tapped on her account. She'd been tagged by @sunshinegirl97 along with the same picture and a similar tagline. "What you should be worried about is if Brynlee sees this. She'll know you bought her an engagement ring."

The smug look on Travis's face disappeared faster than the plate of homemade cookies Presley had delivered to the fire station last night. "Shoot, this is going to ruin the surprise," Travis said, pulling his phone from his pocket. "What are your plans today?"

"What I do every day," Presley said. "Working and training." She held up her phone. "But first, I need to fix this mess."

"I really need your help," Travis said. "I need to ask Bryn to marry me today instead of next week."

"How are you going to that?" Presley asked. "Isn't the fire drill scheduled for next week?"

"Yes, but I'm hoping the principal will let us do it today." He looked at her with pleading eyes. "That's where you come in. Mrs. Trimble will do anything for you."

"Mrs. Trimble wants me to marry her son and get him out of her basement."

Travis laughed, and Presley couldn't say no to her brother. After all, she was the one who had come up with the idea for him to propose to Brynlee during a fire drill at the school where she taught sixth grade. Principal Trimble had agreed to alert the sixth-grade classes of a fire drill in exchange for Travis and his crew coming do an assembly for the school. Travis and his crew would've done the assembly anyway, but this way, he could ask Brynlee to marry him in front of her class. The kids adored her, and so did the other teachers.

"All right, I'll talk to Mrs. Trimble and hope her cooperation isn't contingent on me going out with Damion the basement dweller."

"Just tell her you're engaged," Travis said with a smirk.

Presley opened her mouth to argue then clamped it shut quickly. "Actually, that's not a bad idea."

"I'll get Kade to help me with everything else," Travis said, looking down at his phone as he quickly typed in a message.

"Kade is helping you?" she asked, trying not to sound too interested. Presley had conflicting feelings for Kade Hunter. He was hotter than a California wildfire and just as risky. Presley had crushed on Kade from the first day she'd met him seven years earlier when she was only seventeen. Travis had just started the fire academy and met Kade his first day. The two had become close friends and had gone on to train as paramedics. Now they worked for the Silver Pine fire department, a small community about an hour north of San Diego, California. The two men had been inseparable until

Travis met Brynlee. Kade wasn't very happy that his best friend was about to get trapped into marriage.

"Isn't he totally opposed to you getting married?" she asked when Travis finished his text and looked up from his phone.

"Nah, he loves Brynlee." Travis pocketed his phone. "He doesn't love her the same way I do," he added with a grin. "By the way, he's agreed to be the best man."

Presley silently thanked her brother for asking Kade to be his best man. Since she was sure Brynlee would ask her to be the maid of honor, it meant she and Kade would have to walk down the aisle together and share at least one dance. It was probably the closest she'd ever come to going out with him and with her brother's blessing. Travis was slightly overprotective of her, and all the guys at the station knew she was off-limits.

"I'm glad he's finally supportive," Presley said.

"So," Travis said, leaning back against the countertop, "when can you stop by the school?"

"I'll go right after my morning workout." She looked at her phone. "Then I seriously need to take care of this misunderstanding."

"Stop worrying. Once Brynlee and I are engaged, you can clear things up with your fans."

He had a point. Presley could post pictures of Travis and Brynlee's engagement and explain why she was trying on diamond rings and who the mystery man was in the photo. She would tag Sunshine Girl, and hopefully she would spread the word since she was the one who started this whole mess by posting the picture.

"True." Presley opened the fridge and pulled out a container of egg whites, almond milk, and the Ground Zero protein powder for her pre-workout. "If I have to sacrifice and go out with Damion, then I will," she said with a grimace.

Travis grinned. "Thanks, sis." He pushed away from the countertop and grabbed his duffel. "I don't know what I'd do without you." He pressed a kiss to the top of her head and then headed up the stairs to shower.

Presley sighed, knowing her brother didn't need her. Or, at least, he wouldn't need her once he got married. Although they hadn't set an official date, she knew Travis and Brynlee didn't plan on having a long engagement. The two had only met a few months ago when Travis rescued Brynlee. Her car had broken down, and Travis being Travis stopped to help her. It was love at first sight. The two were so cute together and deserved to be newlyweds without a sister invading their privacy. The three-bedroom townhouse she and Travis lived in was perfect for the two of them, but three would definitely be a crowd.

Her big brother was her hero and had been there for Presley through everything. At eighteen, he'd been forced to become the man of the house when their father was killed in a car accident. Presley was only fourteen at the time. While their father's death had rocked their happy world, it was the discovery of his infidelity that had crushed their small family. Her dad wasn't the only person in the car. The other victim was his mistress.

Presley remembered how devastated her mother was when the police gave her the news about the other woman. Even more devastating, the affair had been going on for years. All those business trips weren't just business. Mark Windsor had had a completely different life in Arizona.

"Mom, I wish you were still here," Presley whispered to herself. She always missed her mom, but at Christmas time, the hurt still felt physical as if Presley couldn't draw in a deep breath until the holiday was over. Her mom had been her hero too. She'd fought to stay with her two children, but cancer was a nasty opponent. It didn't fight fair, sneaking in like a thief and stealing Emily Windsor's life only three years after her husband had died.

If not for Travis, Presley would've gone into foster care. Their father had left them with nothing. He didn't even have a life insurance policy. Mom had worked two different jobs to keep them in their small home. After she died, Travis and Presley had sold the house to pay off medical bills and to pay for their mother's funeral.

Presley was barely seventeen at the time, so her brother had dropped out of college and returned home to make sure she finished high school. Travis gave up his dream to be a doctor and trained to be a firefighter paramedic as an alternative. He'd missed out on so much, including sharing a bachelor pad with Kade.

Guilt weighed heavily on Presley's shoulders. She didn't want to be a burden to her brother anymore. At twenty-three, Presley was old enough to live on her own, but she wasn't in any financial position to afford moving out. She wasn't desperate enough to marry Damion, but she needed to do something. She was a personal trainer and took a few online classes toward a degree in exercise science. She'd toyed with the idea of being a physical therapist, but it required a doctor's degree instead of a master. She didn't even have a bachelor's degree yet.

Her dream job was to work for Ground Zero, one of the top sponsors for *America's Ninja Champions*. Winning the women's division for *Ninja Champions* was the perfect solution to fast-track into the company. The two hundred and fifty thousand grand prize would pay for school and allow her to find a place of her own. The part-time job at Gus's Gym didn't pay much but gave her free access to working out and training.

Presley's debut into the ninja competition last year had gone okay, but she hadn't made it past tier three. If she won the grand prize, it was also a chance for her to pick up endorsements and gain a bigger following. She might even get a chance to be Ground Zero's brand ambassador for their new activewear clothing line.

After Presley downed her protein drink, she called Zuri and left a detailed voicemail about the situation. Just to be safe, she went ahead and sent her a text, asking Zuri to call her as soon as possible. Knowing this would all be cleared up by tomorrow, Presley headed out for the day. She was so excited about finally getting a sister that she stopped by the school first. Mrs. Trimble was in a good mood. Apparently, Damion had met a woman online and was no longer on the market. Presley refrained from dropping to her knees in a prayer of thanksgiving for small miracles. By the time she left for the gym, the fire drill was all arranged to happen right after lunch.

The proposal was epic and worth all the effort. "Let me see the ring on your finger," Presley said, taking Brynlee by the left hand. "Oh my gosh, it's so beautiful!" She hugged her future sister-in-law, and they both squealed like teenagers.

"You helped pick it out, silly," Brynlee said, holding up her hand, so the ring caught the sunlight, making it as sparkly as Brynlee's eyes. "I love it, by the way," Brynlee said. "Sorry about the Instagram post. Did Zuri ever get back with you?"

"Seeing you happily engaged to my brother made it worth it," Presley said, wishing her PR agent was more reliable. "Zuri sent me a text a couple of hours ago that she was working on it." Presley used the term PR agent loosely when it came to the new college grad. But Zuri was all she could afford, which was nothing since the girl needed the experience, and Presley needed someone to give her a presence on social media.

Brynlee looked worried. Presley didn't want to ruin their special day with her problems. "I'm sure she'll have everything figured out," Presley said as Travis and his crew got ready to leave. "Go give Travis a kiss goodbye, and I'll see you at the party tonight."

"Okay," Brynlee said. "Love you." She blew Presley a kiss and then rushed across the yard to say her goodbyes.

Presley turned to head back to her car when she heard a familiar voice. "Hey, Princess Warrior," Kade hollered out. She turned and saw him hanging onto the door of the firetruck. "Need a ride home?"

For just a moment, she wondered what it would be like if he were serious, and she had the right to run into his arms and kiss him like Brynlee kissed Travis. The fantasy bubble popped like an overinflated balloon when she saw the smirk on Kade's handsome face. He probably knew he flustered Presley and was just messing with her.

"Thanks, but I'm good," she said, dangling her car keys. He grinned and waved to her before climbing into the firetruck.

With a sigh, Presley turned away from him and hurried to her car. She knew Kade was coming to the party tonight, so she wanted to shower and find something cute to wear before heading over to the gym to help Gus and his wife with the party.

Hours later, Presley hung back in the shadows of Gus's Gym, watching Travis and Brynlee say goodbye to their friends and family as they filed outside. Gus had closed the gym early for the engagement party, and it had been a success. Gus, a former Navy guy, let the firefighters work out at the gym for free. The gym frequently had emergency vehicles in the parking lot, and tonight was no different.

Presley's gaze drifted to the small snack bar where Gus and his wife had served smoothies. The couple had left a short time ago, leaving the cleanup for Presley to do as soon as the guests were gone. Kade had hung out there most of the night, talking to one pretty woman after another. He was too handsome for his own good. Right now, he was talking to a pretty girl who worked for the county dispatch. She was new and appeared to be a member of the Kade Hunter fan club already.

As if sensing she was watching him, Kade's head turned slightly, and their eyes met. Presley leaned against the wall for support. One look into Kade's silvery-blue eyes made her legs feel like she'd just completed three reps of weighted walking lunges. He made her flustered and irritated at the same time. Out of all of the firefighters, why did her heart have to go haywire whenever Kade looked at her?

A slow, sexy grin curved his mouth, and he winked at her. Presley narrowed her eyes, wishing her body didn't react to his teasing. Because he was teasing her and treated her like a little sister. All of the guys at the station treated her like a little sister.

The pretty redhead he was talking to turned to see what was drawing Kade's attention away from her. She glared at Presley, anger flashing in her green eyes. Presley almost laughed out loud. She was no threat when it came to Kade Hunter. The man enjoyed female attention and was very vocal that he wasn't looking for a long-term commitment in the foreseeable future. Presley wasn't ready for anything serious either. Because of her dad, she had trust issues when it came to men. Besides, she didn't have time for a boyfriend. Travis and Brynlee spent every second they could together. Presley spent every second she had working, meal prepping, and training for the upcoming season of *Ninja Champions*.

Her eyes drifted from the redhead to Kade. Amusement glinted in his eyes as if he wanted to see what would happen between the two women vying for his attention. *Wait...*she wasn't vying for his attention. She cut him a scathing glare of her own, which only increased the laughter in his eyes.

Before Presley did something silly like stick out her tongue at Kade, her phone buzzed inside her back pocket. Turning away, she glanced at the screen and quickly accepted the call. Zuri was finally calling her back.

The only communication Presley had received from her agent was a text telling her to sit tight, asking Presley not to respond to her fans. Not that Presley had that many fans yet. At least not as many fans as her archenemy, Jolene Ivy, otherwise known as Poison Ivy, had. The three-year *Ninja Champion* veteran had a vendetta against Presley after she'd defeated her in the second tier of last season. Jolene was the reason why

Presley accepted Zuri's offer to help her increase her following.

Zuri, Gus's niece, had just graduated with a marketing degree with a focus on social media and digital marketing. Even with a degree, Zuri needed more experience to find a job. Poison Ivy had launched a social media campaign against the Princess Warrior, making it necessary for Presley to fight back. Only she didn't really do social media. She didn't have time for it. Presley had to admit that Zuri was doing a good job getting her name out there. Last year no one really knew who Presley Windsor was or cared whether she was engaged or had a boyfriend. Now thousands of followers wanted to know who Prince Charming was.

"Hey," Presley said. "I'm glad you called."

Zuri interrupted her before Presley could tell her about the pictures of the engagement she wanted to post online. "I have the best news ever!" Zuri said.

"You do?" Presley asked.

"Yes!" Zuri squealed. "Thanks to me, you are going to be one of the contestants featured on the pre-season *Ninja Champion's* kickoff special!"

"Are you serious?" Presley said, letting out a tiny squeal of her own. "I thought they decided that I wasn't going to be on the special?"

To be featured on the special meant the network considered her as a serious contender for the upcoming season. Last month, a cameraman had followed Presley around for a couple of days, getting footage of her daily training routine, where she worked, and what inspired her to become a *Ninja Champion.*

Presley had been so disappointed when she'd learned she hadn't made the cut for the network's kickoff special scheduled to air on New Year's Day.

"After talking to me, they changed their mind," Zuri said with a hint of pride in her voice. "They're very excited to reveal your Prince Charming on national television."

"My what?" Presley asked, shaking her head as if to clear her hearing.

"You know," Zuri said with a light laugh, "your fiancé."

All the air in Presley's lungs expelled in a whoosh, making her dizzy. She reached out for the door handle to Gus's office and held on tightly. "I'm not engaged," Presley choked out.

"Yes, you are," Zuri said. "I've already confirmed it on Insta and Twitter. Didn't you get my message?"

"Yes, you told me to sit tight while you took care of things!" Presley said in a loud voice. She winced, hoping nobody heard her. Glancing over her shoulder, she saw Kade wasn't paying attention to her. She wanted to keep it that way until she figured out this mess. Testing the doorknob, she was grateful it wasn't locked and stepped inside the office, closing the door for privacy.

"I did take care of things, and now you'll be on the special," Zuri said, sounding completely affronted. "You're welcome."

"Zuri." Presley's phone beeped, and her phone asked her how she could help her. She hit the button to clear the screen and started over. "You're not listening to me. I'm not engaged. I don't even have a boyfriend."

"But the picture clearly showed you trying on an engagement ring."

"Right, but the guy in the picture is my brother Travis."

"You're marrying your brother?"

"*What?* No, of course not." Presley let out a frustrated breath. She couldn't fire Zuri because she wasn't paying her anything. "I was helping Travis pick out an engagement ring for his girlfriend. He just got engaged today."

"Are you guys planning a double wedding?" Zuri asked. "Because that might be a cool angle too."

"I. Am. Not. Getting. Married!" Presley said, enunciating each word for emphasis. "I told you this in my voicemail."

"I never check my voicemail," Zuri said. "I just got your text that said you were engaged and somebody leaked it early."

Presley pulled the phone away from her ear and wanted to smack herself in the head with the device. How had Zuri misread the text message? There was no way she had said any of that. Drawing in a fortifying breath, she put the cell to her ear and explained that she planned to post pictures of Travis and Brynlee's engagement to clear up the misunderstanding. Calling it a misunderstanding at this point was an understatement bigger than the San Andreas Fault line, but she couldn't focus on that right now.

"We can still post the pictures of their engagement," Presley said. "It's the only way to fix this mess."

"You can't do that!" Zuri said in a panic. "This will end my career as a PR agent."

Presley bit her tongue, so she didn't say how ending Zuri's career as a PR agent would be a humanitarian service and worthy of the Nobel Peace Prize. "We have to do something because I'm not engaged."

"Have you looked at all the likes and comments on Instagram?" Zuri asked, ignoring the truth. "This is huge for you. The owner of Ground Zero even congratulated you."

Weslee Steele commented on the post? That was a big deal. But the fact still remained that Presley wasn't engaged. "We'll just have to tell them that we broke up."

"You can't do that, either!" Zuri said. "I've been working out the deal with the producers all day long. They want to do a big reveal of who your fiancé is and asked if you and your boyfriend would do a reenactment of the proposal. I sent you an email with all of the information and the contract to sign."

Presley wasn't sure what to say because Zuri wasn't listening. She needed to hang up and talk to Travis. Her big brother would know what to do. "Um, I need to go...but I'll call you later."

"Please don't blow this, Presley," Zuri begged. "Jolene is furious, by the way. She's on the special too and is throwing a fit that they've added you to the lineup."

Oh, man. Why did she have to go and tell her that? "I know, but I still don't have a boyfriend. You get that, right?"

"Are you sure you don't have a boyfriend?" Zuri asked. "Surely someone as gorgeous as you will have a man who is willing to help you out."

Nope, but thank you so much for the reminder. "I'm not in a relationship right now, Zuri." Presley massaged the side of her head. "Listen, before we try to figure this out, I need to talk to my brother."

"Okay." Zuri let out a noisy breath. "Just remember how big this is and what being on the special will do for your career."

"Yep, I'll keep that in mind."

Ending the call, Presley continued to rub the side of her head and thought about checking out the post so she could verify that Weslee Steele had truly liked and commented on her non-existent engagement. But first, she really needed to talk to her brother. Turning around, she startled at the three faces staring at her through the glass window.

Brynlee looked worried. Travis looked frustrated. And Kade looked sexy...er...curious.

CHAPTER 2

KADE

Kade wished he could hear the conversation Presley was having. He could tell she was upset. He almost opened the door to the office but stopped when Travis and Brynlee started coming his way. They'd just said goodbye to the final guest and realized that Presley had disappeared.

"Did you find her?" Travis asked.

"Yeah, she's in Gus's office having a very heated conversation with someone."

"Oh dear," Brynlee said. "I'm sure this has something to do with her fiancé."

All the muscles inside Kade's gut tightened as he turned to look at Travis incredulously. "Presley's engaged?" he asked, hoping his voice didn't reveal the strange feeling of jealousy surging through his bloodstream. What was his deal anyway? Travis's little sister might be a gorgeous blonde goddess with a body meant to be worshipped, but she was off-limits.

Travis made sure every guy at the station understood that. Nobody dared look at Presley as anything but a little sister. Kade remembered the rookie firefighter who must have missed the memo as he vocalized his thoughts about what he'd like to do with Presley. The kid hadn't even finished his lustful sentence before Travis laid him out flat. He moved to another city soon after.

"No," Travis said irritably. "Someone got a pic of her helping me pick out Bryn's ring and assumed she was getting engaged."

Some of the tension ebbed out of Kade's shoulders. "I didn't think she was dating anyone." He slugged Travis in the shoulder. "Not with Big Brother watching."

"You make me sound like a psycho," Travis said, rubbing his shoulder. "I'm just protective."

"Dude, you knocked a rookie firefighter out cold."

"Travis!" Brynlee said with shock. "When did you do this?"

"Thanks a lot," Travis said to Kade. Then he put an arm around his fiancée. "Honey, it was last year, and the guy was saying vile things about Presley."

"Did he know you were her brother?"

Travis shrugged. "I didn't bother asking."

"Violence isn't the answer, Travis," Brynlee said in her sweet, grade-school teacher voice. "Just so we're clear, I love you, but if you ever get thrown in jail, I won't be visiting."

"So, that's a no to conjugal visits?" Travis asked with a teasing smile.

"You are very tempting." Brynlee kissed him on the mouth. "But it's a definite no."

"Stop," Kade groaned. "You guys are killing me."

Travis grinned and leaned in for another kiss. Kade rolled his eyes and turned away from the couple. His friend had fallen into the marriage trap. Once he made his vows, the only way out of it was death or divorce. Both options weren't very good, so Kade planned on avoiding the institution for as long as possible. Maybe in a few years, after he was in his mid-thirties, he'd think about finding a wife. Kade did love kids and wanted a couple of his own. For now, he was content being the most awesome uncle to his nieces and nephews. With three younger sisters all married and procreating, he didn't need to rush into anything.

He returned his attention to Presley. She had her back turned to them and was rubbing the side of her head. "Hey, she's off the phone," he said when he saw Presley end the call.

Travis stepped forward and lifted his hand to knock on the door when Presley spun around and noticed them. Her hazel colored eyes widened with shock as she looked at Travis and Brynlee for a few seconds before settling her gaze on Kade. Something hot flared in her eyes before she blinked and looked away from him.

Suddenly the air felt as combustible as a building engulfed in flames. Just like he'd learned in the fire academy, Kade wanted to get out before it was too late. But a firefighter never left another firefighter alone, and Travis wasn't going anywhere, so neither was Kade.

"What's up?" Travis asked when Presley opened the door and stepped out of the office.

"Oh, nothing much." Presley tossed a lock of her honey-blonde hair over her shoulder. "Just that my public relations agent is completely crazy and announced to the world that I'm engaged."

Kade kept his mouth shut as Travis and Brynlee bombarded Presley with questions. She answered them with her usual snark. Something Kade couldn't help but like. Presley, the Princess Warrior, was sexy and sassy. A deadly combination for any man but especially Kade. He had to keep reminding himself that Presley was off-limits. Travis was his best friend, and he didn't want to do anything to ruin their friendship. That, and he wasn't into long-term commitments. Not until he knew for sure the woman he fell in love with was the one he meant just for him. How he'd ever know that was beyond him.

"I don't know what to do," Presley said. "She thinks I can just go out and snag myself a man in the next twenty-four hours."

"Maybe you can," Brynlee said, tapping a finger to her smiling lips.

"Not likely," Presley said.

"I have an idea," Brynlee said, her grin widening. "You need a fake fiancé!"

"*A what?*" Travis and Presley asked at the same time.

"You know, a fake fiancé."

"Fake as in he doesn't exist?" Presley asked.

"No, fake as in temporary or short-term." Apparently, the grade school teacher was also an avid reader of romance novels. Kade stifled a laugh while she explained where she'd gotten the idea. "I just read this whole romance series about fake fiancés. It's the perfect answer."

"No, it isn't," Presley said.

"Yeah, Bryn," Travis said in a hesitant voice as if he didn't want to offend his girlfriend. "I'm not sure finding her a fill-in boyfriend is the best idea."

"It *is* a good idea," Brynlee insisted. She reached out and took both of Presley's hands in hers. "You said yourself that getting on that special would be an amazing boost and will help you get sponsors like Ground Zero. Just think of the fake fiancé thing more like having a plus one for your interview."

"I guess that could work," Travis said when Brynlee looked at him for backup.

Presley pulled her hands free and started pacing in front of them. Then she stopped and stared at her brother with wide eyes. "Are you being serious right now?" she asked.

Kade wanted to ask Travis the same thing. Obviously, falling in love was making the man stupid. This was precisely why Kade steered clear of relationships that went beyond a couple of dates.

"Well, yeah." Travis shifted on his feet and rubbed a hand across his jaw. "You want to win this, right?" he asked.

"Yes." Presley licked her lips and darted a glance at Kade.

He lifted a questioning brow and shook his head. "Don't do it," Kade whispered in an ominous voice. "They're crazy," he added while twirling a finger around his head.

"Just hear me out," Travis said, cutting Kade a glare before focusing back on his sister. "It seems like every contestant featured on the kick-off special acquires some kind of magical powers. Almost all of them have made it to the final tier."

Kade couldn't believe Presley was actually considering doing this. But as Travis and Brynlee continued talking about her getting noticed by Ground Zero and the potential of becoming the brand ambassador for their new clothing line, he knew she was warming to the idea. He started to shake his head, but Presley wasn't looking at him. She stared steadily at her brother and his fiancée, soaking in every word coming out of their mouths.

"Okay," Presley said, still avoiding looking at Kade, "even if I agree to this insane idea, who is crazy enough to be my fake fiancé?"

"You'll do it?" Travis and Brynlee asked at the same time.

Kade was too stunned to chime in with his opinion. It wasn't like he had a say in what Presley did or didn't do. He certainly knew better than to question Travis when it came to his sister.

"I don't want to." Presley worried her bottom lip. "But I also don't want to lose out on this opportunity."

"Yay," Brynlee said, clapping her hands. "Now we have to find you a fake fiancé."

All the color drained from Presley's pretty face. "Nope, I can't do this," she said, shaking her head. "We have to come up with another plan other than me marrying some random guy."

"You're not actually getting married," Brynlee said. "Remember, he's your plus one, and this is short term."

Just when Kade thought Presley was coming to her senses, she considered Brynlee's words. "Okay, but again, where are you going to find a guy willing to do this?" Presley held out her hands in front of her. "For free," she added. "Because even if we pooled our money together, we wouldn't have enough to hire someone."

"What about Damion?" Brynlee asked. "He's not too bad and would love to help you."

Kade wanted to know who Damion was but kept his mouth shut. Judging from the look on Presley's face, he guessed she wasn't into him.

"First, *eww*. I can't even—just yuck," Presley said with a shudder. "Second, he's not available." She pressed her palms together and looked heavenward. "Thank heaven for small miracles."

"Yeah, we might want to steer clear of obsessive fans," Travis said. "I think we need someone Presley already knows and is comfortable around."

"What about one of the single guys at the station?" Brynlee asked, glancing up at Travis.

"Um, no." Presley shook her head, making her blonde curls ripple across her shoulders. "Absolutely not." She shot Kade a look he couldn't quite read before adding, "Most of the guys are all like brothers to me."

Kade wasn't sure why that statement bothered him so much. He might treat Presley like a little sister but he noticed things about Presley that no brother should ever notice about a sibling. Looking at her sidelong, he studied her profile, appreciating the curve of her cheek and her full bottom lip that had him thinking about what it might feel like to kiss her. See...not brotherly thoughts. *Wait a sec...*she'd said, *"most of the guys."* Did that include him?

"That's not a bad thing," Travis said as a slow smile spread across his face. "Speaking of brothers," he said, shifting his focus on Kade. "I think I know the perfect guy."

"Good idea, babe," Brynlee said, clapping her hands again. "He's perfect."

Kade's skin flushed hot and then cold as Travis and Brynlee pinpointed him as their target. Did they seriously want him to do this? And why in the heck was he still standing here instead of running out the door for safety? He heard Presley gasp and could feel her watching him. He was tempted to look at her, wanting to see if she was as intrigued by the idea as he was.

Intrigued? Yeah, he was intrigued and not opposed to playing the part of her stand-in fiancé. Heck, Kade knew every single guy at the station would jump at the chance to be the Princess Warrior's pretend boyfriend. Apparently, so would he.

CHAPTER 3

PRESLEY

Presley sucked in a sharp breath and stared at Kade, trying to gauge his thoughts. She half expected him to bust out laughing and then hightail it out the door. Travis was nuts if he thought Kade would pretend to be her boyfriend, let alone pretend to be her fiancé on national television. Still, when he didn't protest right away, a minuscule part of her heart hoped he might say yes.

"Dude," Kade said, running a hand through his dark, wavy hair. "Are you asking me to do it?"

"Well, yeah," Travis said. "You're like a brother to her, and Presley is comfortable around you."

Comfortable? All she had to do was look at Kade to become hot and bothered. *And brother?* Please, Presley had never once thought of Kade Hunter as a brother. But crushing on him was as futile now as it was when she was seventeen. Kade was a serial dater, claiming he wasn't in any rush to fall into the trap called marriage. He'd told Travis more than once that if there was a woman out there to make him change his mind, he hadn't found her yet.

"You can't ask Kade to be my fake fiancé," Presley said.

"Why not?" Travis asked.

"Yeah," Kade said with a smirk. "Why not?"

"Because…" *I've been in love with you forever, and you'll break my heart.* "…because you've got a girlfriend."

"Nope," Kade said, winking at her. "Haven't had a girlfriend for a while now."

Presley opened her mouth and then compressed her lips in a flat line. Why was Kade willing to do this? There had to be a catch. "Why would you want to?" she asked, unable to hide the suspicious tone of her voice.

His silvery blue eyes sparked with mischief as his mouth curled deliciously into a sexy half grin. "Because I'm like a brother to you, and I want to help you out."

She barely suppressed a sarcastic snort and wanted to call him out. Even if he didn't know she'd had a crush on him forever, he had to know she didn't view him as a brother.

"This is so perfect!" Brynlee said, giving Presley a quick hug. "It'll be just like a Hallmark Christmas movie."

Presley wished Brynlee would stop calling this whole thing perfect. Besides, she'd watched a lot of those Hallmark movies with Brynlee and knew how they all ended. With the couples living happily ever after. She was about to remind her exuberant future sister-in-law that this relationship was short-term and only for the interview when she remembered Zuri telling her the producers wanted a reenactment of the proposal and then a big reveal of her Prince Charming.

"Oh no," she said, feeling like a piece of bread was stuck in her throat. "I forgot what Zuri said the producers wanted."

"What do they want?" Kade asked, not looking nearly as amused as he was a few seconds ago.

"Let me check the email she sent me." She pulled her phone from her back pocket and tapped on the screen. Scrolling down, she ignored all the unread messages and found Zuri's name.

Opening the email, her stomach twisted like the pulled taffy she and Brynlee had made the week before as she read the legal jargon, which made very little sense to her. Zuri proved more helpful than usual by providing a brief summary of what was expected at the end of the message. Presley didn't usually swear, but a mild curse word slipped out of her mouth, making Brynlee's eyes widen, and Kade and Travis laugh.

"It must be bad," Travis snickered. "Let me see." Her brother snatched the phone out of her hand and started reading the legal crap out loud.

"Read the last paragraph," Presley said. "You'll see why this just got a whole lot more complicated than a plus one."

As Travis read through Zuri's summary, Presley covertly watched Kade's expression slip from entertained all the way down to terrified. He looked up sharply, and their eyes met for several intense seconds.

"They want to film us spending Christmas together?" he asked, his usual olive skin tone looking a little on the green side. "And then reenact our engagement?"

It was silly to get her feelings hurt over his reaction. She felt exactly the same way. Still, seeing his obvious aversion made her want to cry. Presley didn't cry. At least not easily.

"Don't worry about it," she said, feeling hot tears press against the back of her eyes. "I'm not signing any contract." Her voice warbled with unwanted emotion, so she gently cleared her throat. "I'll message Zuri and tell her she needs to fix this mess."

She held out her hand for her phone, but Travis didn't give it to her. Presley recognized the fierce protectiveness on his face. Her brother was the best and hated seeing her hurt. "Hold on a sec," he said, holding it up out of her reach. "Let's talk about this before we make any rash decisions."

"There's nothing to talk about," Presley said. "I'm planning on spending Christmas with you and Bryn at her family's house in Oceanside." She glanced at Kade. "And Travis said you're going home to Santa Monica for Christmas, so that's that."

"Not going home," Kade said, some of the color coming back into his handsome face. "We're spending Christmas at my stepdad's cabin in Big Bear Lake."

"Okay," Presley said, not sure why that mattered. "I hope you have fun."

"Why don't you go with Kade?" Brynlee asked. "I'm sure Kade's family would love to have you."

Presley shook her head so violently that her hair whipped around her face. "They don't know me that well," she said, pushing a strand of her hair behind her ear. In fact, she'd only met Kade's mom once. The woman was beautiful and a little bit scary. Someone as sophisticated as she was wouldn't want someone like Presley for a daughter-in-law. Presley only owned like three dresses. The rest of her wardrobe consisted of jeans, tees, and yoga pants.

Moistening her lips, Presley darted another look at Kade. He was watching her closely, a small smile playing at his mouth. "Can we just forget this?" she asked, hoping he'd readily agree with her.

Before he had a chance to answer her, Brynlee spoke up again. "Trav, is there anyone else at the station who would be willing to do it then?"

"Maybe," Travis said at the same time Kade said a resounding *no*.

Everyone turned to look at him. "What?" Kade said, shrugging his shoulders. "I have Christmas off this year, and my family won't mind if I bring a girl home with me." He grinned. "My sisters will be forced to lay off finding me a girlfriend, so it's a win-win."

"Perfect," Brynlee said for what seemed like the hundredth time tonight. "Okay, so how are you proposing to Presley?"

"Uh, I have no idea." Kade looked uncomfortable again and didn't meet Presley's gaze directly. "I would never do anything as elaborate as you," he said, turning to Travis.

Again, it was silly to get her feelings hurt. This wasn't a real engagement. But someday, if Presley decided to get married, she hoped the man would be just like her brother. And what girl didn't want her future husband to go all out when he proposed?

"You don't have to do anything big, just romantic like maybe sitting in front of the fire or having a nice candlelit dinner,"

Brynlee said. Turning to Travis, she kissed him on the cheek. "Thanks for going all out for me, by the way." She palmed Travis's jaw as she gazed lovingly into his eyes. "I love you so much."

Brynlee's diamond ring caught the overhead light and sparkled like the twinkling lights on the Christmas tree Gus's wife had put up right after Thanksgiving. Shoot, what was Presley supposed to do for a ring? This was getting way too complicated. She couldn't afford to buy a fake engagement ring. Travis couldn't either. She doubted Kade wanted to blow a thousand dollars on a ring.

"I love you too," Travis said before covering Brynlee's mouth with his own.

Everything inside Presley froze as she watched the newly engaged couple kiss. Kissing was a normal thing between two people who loved each other. Did that mean Kade would have to kiss her? More than once? She could barely draw in her next breath as she dared to sneak a look at him and found him watching her again.

"You don't have to do this," Presley said, her voice catching on the last word. "I'll figure something out."

"You're not getting one of the other guys at the station to do it," Kade said, his eyes narrowing with annoyance. "I've got your brother's back, and he's got mine." He smiled, softening the hard lines of his face. "This will help me too. I'm serious when I say my sisters are always after me to get a girlfriend."

"Won't they be upset when you bring home a fiancée instead of just a girlfriend?"

"Nah, they'll be too happy I brought a girl home to be mad at me." He shrugged. "My mom is just as bad and is always pressing me about when I plan on growing up to start a family."

"You've never brought a girl home?" she asked, not sure why that mattered so much to her.

"No, I've brought a few home, mainly to appease my sisters and to keep my mom's matchmaking schemes at bay."

Before Presley could ask him for further details, her cell phone pinged an incoming text. Since Travis still had her phone, he was the first one to read it. "It's from Zuri," he said, scanning the message. "Guess she's pretty confident you're on board with all of this." Travis shook his head and handed Presley the phone. "She wants to know if you've signed the contract yet and what you and your fiancé's plans are for Christmas so she can schedule it with the network."

Presley read over the message again, her mind still stuck on the girls that Kade brought home. He must have liked them enough to let his family meet them. Glancing up, she met Kade's eyes. "Are you sure you don't need to think about this before I reply?"

He considered her for a long moment, a slight wrinkle to his brow. "I want to help you, Presley, but this is your call." He nodded his chin at Travis and Brynlee. "Don't let any of us pressure you into something you don't want to do."

"He's right, sis," Travis said. "This is your call."

Three messages pinged one after another. The first one was a screenshot of Zuri's post about Presley's secret engagement and the big reveal on the kick-off special. It had thousands of likes already and almost just as many comments. The second one showed how many times followers had retweeted the news about the big reveal. The third one was a text from Zuri, begging Presley not to blow this deal. A fourth message came through, followed by a row of praying hands emojis.

Zuri: One of the producers asked if I was willing to move to LA for a job possibility. This is so big for both of us!

It might be Presley's call, but things had escalated so quickly that it was beyond her control. Posting a picture of Travis proposing to Brynlee wasn't going to fix this. Not without making Zuri look totally incompetent. Gus worried about his niece enough as it was. He was so grateful Presley was giving the girl a chance. Kade was willing to help out, plus he said it would benefit him too. So, really, Presley was the one who would get hurt if this whole thing went South.

Making a decision she hoped she wouldn't live to regret, she sent Zuri a message that she would sign the contract electronically. She also added she was spending Christmas in Big Bear, California.

Zuri: Did you find someone to be your fiancé?

Presley: *Yes*

Zuri: Congratulations! I can't wait to meet him.

.   .   .

Dumbfounded, Presley stared at the last message, trying to figure out if Zuri was honestly insane or just incredibly optimistic. Either way, this thing was going down, and there was no way for her to jump ship.

CHAPTER 4

KADE

Without any hesitation, Kade fought fires, scaled mountains, and repelled out of helicopters to rescue people. But taking Presley home for Christmas was more terrifying than any of those things. It was too late to back out now. He'd already committed to pose as her fiancé or her *plus one* as Brynlee liked to refer to it whenever Presley started to panic about the whole thing.

Kade pulled into the visitor's parking space near Presley's condo and cut the engine. He leaned across the passenger seat and unlocked the glove box, taking the black velvet ring box out. He still wasn't sure why he hadn't turned around to take it home. Shortly after he left his condo, Presley texted him that she'd found her mother's wedding ring, so there wasn't a need for him to bring the diamond engagement ring his paternal grandmother had given Kade before she died. The one-carat solitaire was set in a platinum wedding band with a row of diamonds inlaid on either side of the center diamond.

Grandma Hunter had withheld the ring from Neil, her only son, and Kade's birth father when he'd married his high school girlfriend, Marilyn. The circumstances surrounding Kade's parents' marriage wasn't a love match. Kade's mom had gotten pregnant with him her senior year in high school, and Neil Hunter had complained about being trapped in marriage right up until the day he died from an accident on a construction site. Kade had only been five, but even at such a young age, he wasn't too sad about losing his father. Neil was also an alcoholic and a mean drunk.

Grandma Hunter had always been kind. She'd helped out until Kade's mother remarried a year later, and they moved from Nevada to California. His stepdad Ben Miles was amazing, but that didn't make up for how Kade felt about marriage. Still, Grandma Hunter gave Kade the wedding ring that had belonged to her mother and her grandmother before that with the stipulation that Kade only offer it to the girl who he gave his whole heart to.

Kade hadn't found a girl to give the ring to because he wasn't looking for her. Again, he considered returning the ring to his condo, but he was already running late. His mother was expecting him for dinner, and he didn't want to show up late with a surprise fiancée in tow.

Thinking about his mom made Kade's gut clench. He didn't look forward to seeing her face to face. Marilyn Hunter Miles wasn't happy with her only son and his choice to be a firefighter paramedic. Kade knew she'd wanted him to follow in his stepfather's footsteps. Ben Miles owned Miles car dealerships in Nevada and California. Ben was willing to bring Kade in and give him ownership of one of the showrooms, but selling cars wasn't the same thing as saving lives.

Being a firefighter was in Kade's blood. He remembered the exact day he decided it was what he wanted to do when he grew up. When he was only four, he'd been playing in his bedroom when a fire broke out in the kitchen. His dad was drunk again and had fallen asleep, leaving a pan of bacon frying on the stovetop.

Kade remembered hearing the smoke alarm go off. He'd cried out for his dad but was too afraid to leave his room after he opened the door and saw the smoke filling their small house. His mom was working at the 24-hour convenient store, but a neighbor had called 9-1-1. Kade would never forget how terrified he was until a firefighter crashed through the door and rescued him. That was when he knew he wanted to save people when he grew up. Owning a Mercedes car dealership might be more lucrative but the money couldn't compare to saving a life.

His vocation wasn't the only thing Kade's mother didn't like. She wasn't happy that her only son wasn't married to the girl she had set her sights on as a daughter-in-law. Jillian Hastings was the daughter of her mother's best friend. The two women had met right after Kade's mother married Ben, and they moved to Santa Monica. Jillian's parents, Peter and Olivia Hastings, lived across the street. Although the Hastings moved when Jillian and Kade were still in grade school, the two women had remained close. They were like sisters and still got together every week for lunch. For years, Kade and his sisters had called Mrs. Hastings Aunt Olivia and Jillian's dad Uncle Peter. They outgrew the titles, especially when Olivia and his mother decided that Jillian and Kade should get married.

The first time his mom suggested he take Jillian out on a date, Kade had told her it was against the law to date your cousin.

He'd been kidding, but after that, his mother made sure that he addressed Olivia and Peter as Mr. and Mrs. Hastings.

Jillian was pretty and all, and Kade had been attracted to her, but the timing had always been off. Any time their mothers made a big push for them to get together, either Jillian or Kade was dating someone else. They flirted with each other and had been pretty good friends at one time, but they'd drifted apart over the years.

It wasn't until a few years ago that everything changed between him and Jillian. The Hastings had come to the cabin for Christmas, and Jillian had pulled Kade aside and told him that she liked him and wanted to give dating a shot. Kade was already on his mom's bad side because of his career, so he and Jillian agreed to see what might happen between them. They dated for a few months, longer than Kade would've dreamed. Still, Kade wasn't ready to get married. Jillian told him that she would wait for him, but Kade knew he didn't love her like that. He hadn't like hurting her feelings, but Jillian deserved to be married to someone who really loved her. Jillian may have accepted it, but his mother and Mrs. Hastings never had. They still held out hope their children would eventually get together.

Now Kade was bringing home Presley as his fiancée, and he hoped his mother would be kind. She could be a little intense and didn't like not getting her way. At least he knew the Hastings wouldn't be spending Christmas with them this year. His mom told him Mr. and Mrs. Hastings had decided to fulfill a life-long dream to spend Christmas in Bruges, Belgium. Last he heard, Jillian had a serious boyfriend, and they were going with her parents.

Snapping the lid closed, Kade locked the ring back in the glove box and got out of his SUV, making his way to the condo Presley shared with her brother. The door swung open before he had a chance to knock.

Travis greeted him with a quick embrace that involved a firm pat to his shoulder. "Come on in," Travis said, stepping out of the way for Kade to come inside. "Presley is almost ready."

"Are these all hers?" Kade asked, sidestepping a rolling suitcase and two large duffle bags sitting in the entryway.

"Just the roll-on and red duffle," Travis said. "The black duffle is mine. Brynlee and I are heading out as soon as you and Presley take off." His friend glanced at his watch. "We need to leave soon before afternoon traffic gets too bad."

"Traffic is always bad," Kade said with a chuckle. "You nervous about meeting Brynlee's parents?"

"No, I've video chatted with them a few times, and they love me. It'll just be weird not having Presley with us." A funny looked crossed Travis's features as he held Kade's gaze for a few uncomfortable seconds. "You'll take good care of her, won't you?"

"Yeah, man," Kade said, not liking the critical look on Travis's face. Whatever his friend was about to say, Kade had a feeling he wouldn't like it. "You know I will."

Travis nodded his head, but the intensity of his stare didn't lessen any. "I was thinking that maybe we should establish a few rules."

"Rules?" Kade asked in a tight voice. He wanted to remind Travis that this whole fake fiancé thing wasn't his idea. "Like what?"

"No handsy stuff."

"Give me some credit," Kade said irritably. "Looking out for your sister means I'm not going to get all handsy with her."

"Okay." Travis's jaw tightened as he shifted on his feet. "But I don't think you need to kiss Presley."

"Travis!" a chorus of female voices said from behind him. Kade glanced up and saw both Brynlee and Presley standing at the top of the stairs. Neither one of them looked happy.

"What?" Travis said defensively. "You can still be engaged without kissing."

First of all, Kade hadn't consciously considered the benefits being engaged would give him, but he had to admit that kissing Presley was something he wouldn't mind experiencing. Second, he wanted to remind Travis about how often he and his fiancée kissed. It was like their lips were magnetized and it was impossible not to touch their mouths together whenever they were in close proximity.

"Honey," Brynlee said as she descended the stairs to stand next to Travis. "We want this to be believable, right?"

"Yeah, I guess," Travis said, still not looking like he agreed when he met Kade's gaze again. "Okay, so kissing but no tongue."

Kade wasn't violent by nature, but his fingers curled into a fist as he considered slugging his best friend for the first time since he'd met him. Travis knew Kade didn't mess around with girls for fun, so why was his friend acting like he was some kind of womanizer?

"I cannot believe you just said that," Presley said, punching Travis in the arm with a closed fist. Kade grinned when Travis winced and rubbed his arm. He hoped it hurt.

"Hey, I'm just looking out for you," Travis said, still rubbing his arm.

"Just shut up," Presley said, barreling past her brother and heading toward the kitchen. Her voice cracked, making it sound like she was on the verge of tears. Kade wasn't sure he'd ever seen Presley cry. She was as tough as she was beautiful.

"Travis!" Brynlee said, pinning him with a glare she probably used on her students. It wasn't that scary, but it was apparent she was irritated with her fiancé. "What has gotten into you?" She shot Kade an apologetic look. "Just ignore him. He's kind of being an idiot right now."

"Hey," Travis said with a chuckle. Brynlee put her hands on her hips and narrowed her eyes, daring him to protest further. "Okay," he said, holding up his hands in surrender, "I'm an idiot."

"Yeah, you are!" Presley shouted from the kitchen. Then they heard the backdoor slam shut.

"Apologize to your friend." Brynlee pointed to Kade. "Then load Presley's luggage while I go and talk to her."

"Sorry," Travis said to Brynlee. Her lips thinned, and she pointed to Kade again before whirling around to go and find Presley.

Kade's pulse ticked at a steady rate as he reigned in his anger. He couldn't remember ever feeling this irked at Travis. The two men had bonded from the first day they'd met at the fire academy. They'd even started a deck-building business on the side to supplement their incomes and had never once had any kind of conflict.

"Dude, I'm really sorry," Travis said, rubbing his hand across the back of his neck. "It just seems wrong for my best friend and my little sister to be making out."

"Who said anything about making out?" Kade growled, feeling his anger ratchet up a notch. "Look, Travis, I get that you're protective of Presley, but if you want her focus segment to be real and appealing to the audience, then you'll have to trust me with your little sister."

"You're right." Travis sighed heavily. "I'm sorry, and I do trust you." He held out his hand for Kade to shake.

Setting aside his anger, Kade nodded his head and took his hand, gripping it just tight enough to let Travis know he could take him if he wanted.

"Truce?" Travis asked with a half grin.

"Truce." Kade started to let go, but Travis pulled him in for a man-hug.

"Thanks for not taking my head off," Travis said as he let go and stepped back. "Don't think I've seen you that ticked off before."

"Don't think I've ever been that ticked off before, either," Kade said.

They both turned when they heard Brynlee call out for Presley before hearing the click of the door close. "Let me load these," Kade said, picking up the duffle and grabbing the roll-on with his other hand. "You better go make amends with the women in your life or your Christmas is going to totally suck."

Travis laughed and opened the door for Kade. "Yeah, I don't think Brynlee has ever been that mad at me." He wiggled his eyes eyebrows up and down. "It was kind of hot."

Kade just shook his head and made his way to his SUV. If he ever fell in love, he promised himself he wouldn't go all stupid like Travis. After loading Presley's luggage into the back, he leaned against the side of the car and waited to see if Presley was still coming home with him.

He thought he heard Travis and Presley arguing, but there was too much noise coming from the group of kids unloading a Christmas tree from the back of a truck parked nearby. After several minutes had passed, Kade debated about heading around back to see what was going on.

He made it to the sidewalk when Brynlee and Travis rounded the corner, holding hands and looking like they'd made up from their fight. "Everything good?" he asked, looking beyond them for any sign of Presley.

"Yeah, Presley will be out in a second," Brynlee said. "She went inside to grab her purse."

The front door of the condo opened, and Presley stepped out. Kade's breath hitched when he got a good look at her. With Travis's stupid dating stipulations, he hadn't noticed how she was dressed. Kade was used to seeing her in workout clothes, but for some reason, the fitted long-sleeve tee accentuated her curves in a way that had him glad Travis couldn't read his mind. The dark wash jeans were strategically ripped, exposing hints of her smooth skin, and the half-boots had enough heel that it made her legs look even longer. Basically, she looked hot, and Kade knew he was in trouble.

Maybe those rules weren't such a stupid idea after all.

CHAPTER 5

PRESLEY

Still reeling with embarrassment from Travis's ground rules, Presley avoided direct eye contact with Kade as she came outside. Quite frankly, she was shocked he was still here and willing to go through with this.

"Hey," Travis said when she attempted to walk past him. She hadn't quite forgiven him and needed time. But his hand on her arm made her pause. "Don't be mad," he said, his eyes pleading with her to forgive him. They didn't argue often, and she usually didn't hold a grudge. This time, it was harder to let go of her anger. She knew the reason why had everything to do with crushing on Kade and knowing that this really was just a big favor to her brother, and he was just looking out for her.

"I'm trying not to," she said in a low voice.

Travis let out a long breath and glanced at Kade. "Things are cool with Kade and me, but I can't say goodbye if you're still mad."

Several beats of silence passed as Presley tried to muster up the words. Why couldn't she just let it go? Again, it all came back to Kade, and how he hadn't given any indication that he viewed her as anything more than a sister. She'd hoped that he might have told Travis that he was attracted to her and then ask permission to see if this fake relationship could turn into something more. But no. He'd made it clear that he would take care of her in Travis's absence. Like a brother.

The tension broke when Brynlee started singing the song from the animated show *Frozen*. She sounded just like Elsa as she belted out the lyrics to "Let it Go" with perfect pitch. Singing wasn't one of Presley's talents, but Brynlee sang and played the piano. She was pretty much the perfect woman because she could cook too.

"All right," Presley said with a giggle. "I forgive you."

Travis wrapped her up in his arms and held her close. "I love you, little sister."

"I love you too." She squeezed him hard before releasing him to hug Brynlee. "I love you so much and can't wait until you're officially my sister."

"Ditto." Brynlee held on for a moment later, waiting as Travis meandered over to stand by Kade. Once he was out of earshot, she whispered in Presley's ear. "I hope you get to break Travis's rule for kissing. I'd bet my meager teacher's salary that Kade Hunter knows how to kiss a woman thoroughly."

Presley wanted to smack the back of Brynlee's head for putting such ideas into her head. She was having a hard enough time trying not to let her imagination run wild, and now she wanted to test Brynlee's theory about Kade's kissing skills.

"Thanks for the visual," Presley said dryly. She darted a quick look at Travis and Kade. They were crouched down, inspecting the front tire on Kade's Forerunner. "You," she said, looking back at Brynlee, "are officially on Santa's naughty list."

"I already got what I want for Christmas," Brynlee said, wiggling the ring finger on her left hand. The half-carat diamond Travis bought his future bride winked in the sunlight.

Presley looked down at the ring on her finger. It was her mother's wedding ring, and the diamond wasn't very big, nor was the clarity that good. But it had belonged to her mother, and it made Presley feel close to her.

"Maybe someday I will too," Presley said, tucking the tips of her fingers into her jeans pocket. Seeing the shocked look on Brynlee's face, Presley quickly added, "Someday like in five or ten years."

"*Right*," Brynlee said, sneaking a look toward the men.

"He's my plus one," Presley reminded Brynlee.

"Uh, huh," Brynlee said, patting Presley lightly on the back. "You just keep telling yourself that."

Travis and Kade stood up and looked their way, preventing Presley from coming up with a snarky reply. It was just as well since her mind went blank the second her eyes locked with Kade's baby blue's. *Oh boy, why did the man have to be so beautiful?*

"We better hit the road," he said, his mouth edging up into a crooked smile. "I got a weather alert that Big Bear might get snow this afternoon, and I'd like to get to the cabin before it hits."

"Do you need me to drive?" Presley teased. She was a horrible driver when it came to snow and ice. The two times she'd wrecked, Kade was one of the first responders.

"Hard pass," Kade said with a low chuckle. "I've seen your driving skills."

Feeling like things were back to their normal banter, she hugged Brynlee and Travis one more time before climbing into the passenger seat. She inhaled the scent of Kade's cologne and sighed heavily as she watched him cross in front of the SUV.

Dang. He smelled so good. How was she supposed to survive a three-hour drive without drooling all over him?

Kade got in behind the wheel and started the engine. The radio blasted a rock song from the '70s. "Sorry," Kade said, turning the volume way down. "I forgot you hate my music."

"I don't hate it." Presley reached out and changed the station to country. "I just like this better."

"Hey," he said, changing the station back. "Road-tripping rule number one. The driver is in control of the music."

Presley couldn't believe he was bringing up rules after Travis's demented rules about kissing and keeping his hands to himself. She pressed her lips together, keeping her sarcastic reply inside. "What about a compromise?" Presley asked as Kade pulled out of the parking lot.

"I'm listening," he said, looking at her briefly when he checked to see if the road was clear.

"Since Christmas is only a few days away, let's listen to Christmas music."

"That sounds fair." He pressed on the accelerator and pulled out onto the road. "I have a great playlist on my phone."

"So do I," Presley said, feeling extra sassy. It wasn't that time of the month, but her hormones were all whacky because of Kade and his yummy scented cologne. "And it's not all country music so you can relax."

"Road-tripping rule number two. I reserve the right to veto your choice of music at any time."

"What's up with all the rules?" she asked, feeling more and more defiant. "First Travis and now you."

That shut him up. Presley suppressed a giggle as she watched the tips of Kade's ears turn red. When he remained quiet, she considered toning the snark down a little. He was doing her a favor, as well as her brother.

Before she spoke up, Kade cut a quick look her way. "I guess we need to talk about a few things."

If he asked her how she preferred to be kissed, she was making him take her home right now. "Like what?" she asked, feeling her heartbeat reach optimal cardio without any exercise.

"Our story." He came to a stoplight and turned to look at her. "Like how long we've been dating. That kind of thing."

"Oh, yeah." Her mouth went dry when Kade's eyes dropped to her lips and lingered there for a few seconds. "That's a good idea," she said in a hoarse voice when he looked at her again.

She'd read a few of Brynlee's romance novels and had always scoffed when the author referred to smoldering eyes. But Kade's eyes were smoldering. And it was making Presley want to lean across the center console and press her mouth to his.

The car behind them honked their horn, breaking the moment that should've been awkward but wasn't. Kade lifted a hand and waved at the impatient driver before proceeding through the intersection. Simmering tension filled the atmosphere, making it difficult to draw in a full breath as Kade navigated through traffic and merged onto the freeway, heading northbound for Big Bear Lake.

A Christmas classic rock song played on the stereo, easing some of the tension. "So about our story," Presley said after a few minutes had passed. "We need to stick as close to the truth as possible."

"Like I'm your brother's best friend." Kade looked at her briefly before glancing over his right shoulder to merge in the fast lane. "And we just kind of fell in love?"

Presley was glad he wasn't looking at her. It gave her time to school her emotions. As far as she was concerned, that was pretty darn close to the truth. Kade was her brother's best friend, and she had fallen in love with him. "Right," she said when he took another quick look at her. "Sounds good to me."

"What was our first date?" Kade asked as he returned his attention back on the road.

Since Presley rarely dated, she blurted out one of the few activities she'd ever done. "We went to a movie?"

"Really? That was our first date?" Kade asked with a low chuckle. "I'm usually more creative than that."

An unwelcome feeling of jealousy pinched at Presley's heart at the idea of Kade's dating prowess. "Okay, then what did we do on our first date?"

"Hmm," Kade said, drumming his fingers on the steering

wheel, "I usually like to plan the date around the girl's interests. Like if she's into music, then I'd take her to a concert. Or if she likes to cook, then maybe sign up for a cooking class together."

Envy shot through her like an arrow piercing the bullseye. *He put that much effort into a first date?* It took every ounce of control not to ask him for more details. At least she could ask him one of her burning questions since they were trying to make their relationship as legit as possible.

"What about me?" she asked, looking down at the small diamond on her left hand. "What kind of date would you plan if you were taking me out for the first time?"

"Axe throwing," he said, without thinking about it too long.

Presley's head shot up, and she stared at him with disbelief. "Axe throwing?" she asked, wondering if Brynlee or Travis had ever said anything to Kade about her wanting to try out the sport.

"Yeah, that or maybe going to an archery range for target practice."

Swallowing hard, Presley licked her lips and nodded her head. She loved archery too. Dang, Kade was even better than she'd dreamed. How on earth was she going to stop herself from falling more in love with him than she already was? He turned and caught her watching him and knew she needed to knock it off if she didn't want to give away her feelings for him.

"Either of those sounds like the perfect first date," she said, hoping he didn't hear the catch in her voice. "But let's go with axe throwing, which I'm sure I kicked your butt."

A slow smile tugged at his lips before he looked back at the road. "You think so?" he asked with a throaty laugh that made her skin prickle with goosebumps.

"Yeah, I know so." She didn't really know if she was any good or not. It was too expensive, and she didn't have extra money to waste on axe throwing when she had to save for her own apartment.

"All right, then I'll be sure and set something up."

Set something up? Like for a first date or for their fake engagement date?

"There are a few places nearby my stepdad's cabin," Kade said before Presley got a word out. "I'll bet my sisters and brothers-in-law would like to come too."

Presley had almost forgotten they were spending Christmas with other people. A crushing feeling pressed down on her chest as anxiety twisted her insides into knots. "How many sisters do you have again?"

"Three, and they're technically my half-sisters," Kade said, changing lanes to pass a particularly slow truck in front of them. "Allison is married to Cody, and they have two kids. Lucas is six, and Brooklyn is four."

"Allison, Cody, Lucas and Brooklyn," Presley said. "Got it."

"Next are the twins."

"Twins?" Presley interrupted. "Are they identical?"

"Nope, Jamie has dark hair and brown eyes. Stacie is blonde with blue eyes." He glanced over at Presley. "She actually looks like she could be your sister and not mine."

"Jamie and Stacie," Presley said. "And they're both married?"

"Yep, Jamie is married to Devon, and they have three kids." He started to rattle off their names, sex, and age, but Presley stopped him before he finished.

"Wait, I'm never going to keep them straight." She pulled out her phone and opened her Notes app. "I need to write this down, or I'll never remember names and who belongs to who."

She quickly typed in what she remembered and was ready for the rest. Kade told her about Jamie and Devon's three kids. A boy and two girls—twins, only they were identical. It was clear he enjoyed his role as an uncle, and Presley looked forward to seeing him in that capacity.

"So Blake is three, and the twins are five?" she asked, typing in the information. "Jenny and Laura are their names, right?"

"Yeah," Kade said with a laugh. "You know you don't have to remember everyone's names."

"I know, but I'd think as your fiancée I would at least be familiar with their names." She finished typing and was ready for the last sister.

"My fiancée," Kade said, his voice cracking slightly. "That sounds so..."

So what? Horrible? Great? "Awful?" Presley guessed, feeling like someone had stabbed her heart with a jagged piece of glass.

"Not awful," he said, shooting her a questioning look. "I was going to say it sounds strange."

Strange? "Gee, thanks so much," Presley said dryly. "Just what every girl likes to hear about themselves."

Kade laughed. "I didn't mean it that way." He lifted one shoulder up. "It's just weird—"

"Not much better," Presley said, cutting him off.

"I'm not used to saying fiancée is all," Kade said, glancing at her with that crooked sexy smile of his. "Trust me, I do not think you are weird or strange."

Presley's heart sputtered and then took off again. Good heavens, was the entire week going to be like this? She needed to get a hold of her emotions, so they didn't keep bouncing all over the place like an unruly ping pong ball. She desperately wanted to ask him what he did think about her but decided it was territory she wasn't prepared to venture into just yet. Instead, she asked him about his other sister.

"Yeah, so Stacie is married to Greg, and they have a four-year-old daughter named Maddie. Stacie is five-months pregnant with another girl, but I have no idea what they're naming her."

Presley typed in the information, overwhelmed as she read through the text. "Your family is huge," she said, wondering how she would ever tell them apart. "Do you have any pictures of them?"

"Good idea." Kade kept one hand on the steering wheel and dug his phone from his pocket, handing it to Presley. "We had a family pic done at Thanksgiving, so it's pretty new."

"I thought you had to work Thanksgiving?"

"My brother-in-law's a pro at photoshop and added a picture of me after."

"Impressive." Presley tapped on the screen. "You'll have to unlock it," she said, offering the phone back to him.

"The passcode is F-I-R-E or 3-4-7-3," he said, passing another slow vehicle.

Presley was too stunned to do anything but stare. She knew it was stupid, but sharing a passcode with someone other than family seemed intimate. But then again, Kade said she was like a little sister so it probably didn't mean anything.

"Did you get that?" he asked, cutting her a sidelong look.

"Um, yeah." Presley ducked her head and tapped in the numbers. It felt strange navigating his home screen. The icons were familiar to hers but in a different order and not grouped like she had hers. While searching for the photo app, she noticed he had a couple of unread messages. The nosy part of her wanted to see who was messaging him. But snooping around would officially make her strange or weird. "Where should I look?" she asked, still not seeing the photo app.

"Middle, left side of the screen."

Presley spotted it and opened the app. Even though Kade was sitting next to her and had given her permission, it felt like she was invading his privacy. Selecting recent photos, she tapped on the icon and stared at Kade's family. It was even more overwhelming since her family pics consisted of her and Travis.

"Your mom is beautiful," Presley said, focusing on the matriarch smiling brightly with her large family surrounding her along with a distinguished looking man that was Kade's stepfather. "She doesn't look old enough to be a grandmother."

"Flattery will get you very far with my mother," Kade said with more fondness than sarcasm. "And you can thank her plastic surgeon for her youthful appearance."

"Not sure you're supposed to reveal that kind of stuff," Presley said, zooming in on the sister with blonde hair. Kade was right. Stacie could pass as Presley's sister. Sliding her finger across the screen, she noticed the two sisters with darker hair. They looked more like Kade, only they both had brown eyes. A delicious current of awareness swept over her when her eyes landed on Kade. He was photogenic, something she already knew from the photos of him on the fire department's Facebook page and Instagram account. Kade and Travis were both a favorite of the ladies. For years, followers had been after the fire department to put out a sexy firefighter calendar. Presley wouldn't mind an entire calendar featuring Kade. Seeing her brother like that would be wrong, though. "I won't tell your mom you said that," Presley added. "No need to get on her bad side."

"I've been on her bad side for a while now, but thanks," Kade said dryly but with an added hint of annoyance that drew Presley's attention.

"Why are you on her bad side?" she asked, shifting her focus from the family picture to look at his profile. A shadow of dark whiskers covered his firm jawline, and she saw the muscle in his cheek flex as he delayed answering her question for several seconds.

"She isn't happy with my career choice," he finally said.

"Because it's dangerous?" Presley asked, even though she suspected there was more to the story than just his job.

"Not exactly," Kade said hesitantly. "Let's just say she thinks I could be making more money selling cars."

"That's probably true," Presley said.

Kade cut a quick glance at her with one eyebrow raised. "Mercenary much?"

"No, just being honest," she said with a light laugh. "But making money isn't everything. Not everyone can do what you and Travis do. I feel like your job is more like a calling than a career."

Heat bloomed in Presley's cheeks when Kade looked at her again for one intense heartbeat. In that brief moment, she saw a look of surprise and gratitude. However, it was the burning admiration that made her breath catch and gave her hope that maybe Kade Hunter saw her as more than just his best friend's little sister.

CHAPTER 6

KADE

Not sure if his voice would give him away, Kade took a minute before giving Presley a response. He was already fighting the undercurrent of chemistry flowing between them and didn't need another reason to like her, but Presley's analogy blew him away. Being a firefighter was a calling. He'd just never heard it put quite like that before.

"You're very wise for one so young," he said, not sure why he added the last part about her age. Maybe to remind him she was Travis's baby sister and off-limits.

"I'm not that young," Presley said, sounding completely offended.

Kade knew she was right, but her age was one of the barriers he'd put up the first time he'd noticed Presley wasn't a little girl anymore. "How old are you anyway?" he asked, even though he knew exactly how old she was. It seemed like a good way to move onto a new subject. He didn't want to delve any deeper into his mother's reasons why making money was so important. Reasons like snagging the kind of affluent wife his mom had in mind for him. "And when's your birthday. I should probably know that kind of stuff if we're engaged."

"I'm twenty-three, and if you don't remember my birthday, then maybe we should call off the engagement."

The snark was back in her voice, making Kade smile. Of course he knew when her birthday was. It was the day before his. "March twenty-fourth," he said, glancing over at her as he checked to see if the lane was clear. He needed to take the next exit to get gas and take a bathroom break. "It will be your golden birthday."

"Oh, wow, it will be my golden birthday," she said with a smile in her voice. "I guess you're not such a bad boyfriend, after all."

"Thanks," he said, veering off to the right and slowed down for the exit. He didn't have much experience in the boyfriend department. Other than Jillian, he'd never allowed himself to date a girl long enough to earn the title. "I'm stopping for gas, but we can get something to eat if you're hungry."

"I'm not very hungry, but feel free to grab something if you want." She still had his phone and startled when it pinged an incoming text. "Um, you have a new message on top of your other messages."

"Is it from my mother again?" he asked, making a right turn toward a gas station. His mom had sent him two messages this morning. Without opening them, Kade saw enough of the texts to know his mom wanted him to pack a suit and tie to wear in case they ate dinner at the lodge. Their family had never eaten at the lodge. Not with all of the little kids. He was sure his mom was plotting something but had no idea what it was.

"No, it's from Stacie." Presley held up his phone. "She says you need to call her right away."

"Aw man," Kade said as he waited behind a line of cars turning into the crowded gas station. "I really hope it's not the baby." Stacie had miscarried at ten weeks before this pregnancy. None of them had worried because she was so far along this time. It would be so devastating to lose the baby now.

"I hope not either," Presley said, worrying her bottom lip.

Once Kade was in line for one of the gas pumps, he took his phone back from Presley and opened the message so he could read the full text. Relief flooded through him when Stacie added at the end that it wasn't an emergency and the baby was fine. "It's not the baby," Kade said, glancing over at his passenger. "She probably wants to know why I haven't returned my mom's texts."

"Is there a reason why you haven't responded?" Presley asked. "Not that it's any of my business," she said when Kade glanced up and met her pretty eyes.

"No reason other than I read enough of her text to know answering her would lead to more and more demands that didn't involve just my wardrobe."

A wrinkle of worry creased Presley's smooth forehead. "What about your wardrobe?"

It occurred to him that if they were attending a formal dinner, then his date would need to know about that. What if Presley hadn't packed a dress? They'd both decided the proposal wasn't going to be formal. Before he had a chance to ask her, his cell started ringing. "It's Stacie, so I better answer."

Presley unclicked her seatbelt. "I think I'll run to the bathroom and give you some privacy." She didn't need to leave but he let her go in case she was in dire need of the restroom.

Kade tapped on the screen and then hit the speaker icon. "Hey, I just stopped for gas and was about to call."

"Oh good," Stacie said in a stage-whisper. "I was going to tell you to pull over so you don't wreck when I tell you what Mom's done."

Kade's stomach bottomed out like he'd just jumped out of an airplane. His gut feeling that his mom was up to something had been correct. "What has she done?" he asked, letting off the gas to move ahead a space.

"She invited Jillian to spend Christmas with our family."

A curse word slipped out of Kade's mouth that he quickly apologized to his sister for. "Are you kidding me?" he asked, glancing out the window to make sure Presley wasn't coming back. "I thought she and her boyfriend were going to Belgium with her parents?"

"I guess she broke up with her boyfriend and didn't want to be the third wheel," Stacie said. "Mom is all giddy about Jillian being free and is determined to make you fall in love with her. Allison and Jamie told me not to call you, but I didn't want to blindside you."

Air hissed through Kade's clenched teeth as he bit back another swearword. He had no idea what would happen when he came home with a girlfriend. No, a fiancée. His mother would totally lose it. How could he subject Presley to that kind of thing? "Thanks for the heads up," Kade said, truly appreciating his youngest sister.

"Don't you dare tell me you're not coming now," Stacie said as if she could read Kade's thoughts. "That's why Jamie and Allie didn't want me to say anything. We missed you at Thanksgiving, and the kids are dying to see their favorite uncle."

"This really sucks," Kade said with a humorless laugh. "The you-know-what is gonna hit the fan when I introduce you all to my fiancée."

It was his sister's turn to swear. Hearing it made Kade start to laugh. "Does your husband know you use that kind of language?"

"Where do you think I learned it from?" Stacie asked irritably. "Now be quiet and please explain yourself."

"Well, I'm engaged." The car in front finished with the pump, so Kade pulled forward and cut the engine. "What else is there to explain?"

"Um, maybe like who she is and where you met her and when this happened?" There were a few colorful words interjected in between, which made him question how safe it was to proceed with his journey. His sister wasn't typically so rude or demanding. Kade cut her some slack since it was probably pregnancy hormones messing with her usually sweet personality.

"I was planning on it being a surprise."

"Yeah, mission accomplished." She let out a big breath. "Sorry about all the cussing. I'm not usually a total witch."

"It's okay, Stacie." Kade switched the phone from speaker and climbed out of the car to open the fuel door. "Do you need me to bring chocolate to tame the beast?"

"Ha ha," she said with a small laugh. "But yeah, chocolate will help. I'm craving chocolate covered cinnamon bears, and Greg forgot to look for some when he went out earlier."

"I'll see what I can do," Kade said, swiping his credit card. Since he couldn't explain the real story about his engagement, he did what Presley suggested and stuck as close to the truth as possible.

"Shut up," Stacie said with a breathy laugh. "Are you telling me you're the Princess Warrior's mystery Prince Charming?"

Crap. Kade hadn't counted on his family knowing about any of that. He wasn't sure why since they were always on social media. Plus, they were fans of Presley. "I guess you could say that."

"Oh my heck, Kade. Mother is going to have a coronary."

"I know CPR," he said dryly.

"And Jillian is…I don't know what she's going to do."

"I'm sure Jillian will be happy for me once I announce I'm engaged."

Stacie snorted a loud guffaw. "Kade, she and Mom have been plotting how to get you two back together. I think they've even planned the wedding, so a little thing like you being engaged isn't going to get in their way."

"You're not helping, sis," Kade said, looking through the tinted glass to see if Presley was coming yet. The coast was still clear, giving him a little more time to figure out what to do.

"Jillian and I tried dating, and it didn't work out," Kade said. "Why does she think I've changed my mind?"

"Because Mother is convinced you two belong together. She's got Jillian all excited again."

"I don't understand why Jillian is going along with her," Kade muttered under his breath.

"Well, you did reject her," Stacie said. "Plus, you're kind of hot. At least all my girlfriends tell me that all the time."

"Thanks. I think." Kade finished filling the gas tank and waited for his receipt before getting back inside the car. "I still don't get why she didn't go to Belgium with Mr. and Mrs. Hastings." Seriously, everything just got really complicated. He didn't want to hurt Jillian's feelings, but he couldn't let Presley down.

"I don't understand it either," Stacie said. "Belgium makes incredible chocolate."

Kade laughed. "I promise to bring you chocolate."

"And that's why you're my favorite brother."

"I'm your only brother."

"True." Stacie sighed. "I wish you would've told any of us that you were in a serious relationship. Mom may have still invited Jillian since she's an only child and has no one to spend the holidays with, but they wouldn't have their hopes up that you two might finally get together."

Ah man. Now that his sister put it that way, he knew he couldn't ask Jillian to leave. "I feel sorry for her too, but it doesn't mean I'm in love with her."

"Ahh, I can't believe my brother is in love," Stacie teased. "When are you all getting married?"

Married? Kade swallowed hard, feeling like a pill was stuck in his throat. He almost denied he was getting married but then remembered that's usually what happened once someone got engaged. "I don't know." He swallowed again. "We haven't decided yet." He didn't like lying and had to remind himself that he was doing this for Presley. Kade helped people. It's what he did every day he was on the job.

"Well, it better be soon. I look cute-pregnant right now, but I know I'm going to pop any day now."

"We just got engaged, so it's not happening anytime soon," Kade said, feeling a cold sweat break out on his forehead.

"Shoot, that means I'll probably look huge. Nursing does the opposite to me, and I can't lose weight until I wean the baby. My boobs will be big too."

"Geez, Stace, thanks for the TMI." Kade shook his head. Sometimes his sisters forgot he was a guy and not married. They frequently discussed their menstrual cycle and other women things that he didn't want to know about.

"Sorry," she said with a laugh. "I guess we can discuss dates when you all get here."

"Please don't," he said, seeing Presley standing at the register. "We plan on taking things really slow."

"You're no fun."

Kade knew his sisters would be all over him about setting a wedding date. He needed to get their minds on something else. "Hey, so I will need your help. The network wants to film me proposing to Presley Christmas Eve."

"I thought you already proposed?"

"Yeah, but they want it live." With the time crunch, the producers decided they had would only film the proposal. "Presley and I don't want anything elaborate, just romantic."

"How did you propose to her the first time?" Stacie asked. "Just do a repeat."

Yeah, that wasn't going to work. Not sure America would find the fake fiancé thing very romantic. "It just kind of happened."

"Kade, that's terrible. Every girl deserves an awesome proposal."

Presley was coming out the doors, so Kade quickly finished up the conversation. "Hey, I need to get on the road before the snow hits." He waved at Presley. "Keep this on the down-low, and then we'll talk about it when we get there."

"I'm so excited," Stacie said with a girly squeal. "Oh, and don't forget my chocolate covered cinnamon bears."

"Got it." Ending the call, Kade climbed out of the car. "Hey," he said, coming around to open the passenger door for Presley. "I need to run inside for a minute and get something for Stacie."

"Is she okay?" Presley asked as she brushed past him. His body buzzed from the brief contact as the subtle flowery scent that was all Presley wafted on the air. "I was worried about her," she said, settling onto the seat.

"She's good." Kade knew he had to tell Presley about Jillian and that his mother's obsession that he marry her. He wasn't sure what she would do but guessed Presley would make him take her home. He decided not to tell her until they were closer to the cabin. "Yeah, just craving chocolate and needs a fix."

Presley's full lips parted into a sweet smile. "I totally get that, and I'm not even pregnant."

Hearing her talk about being pregnant someday triggered some repressed fantasy. As if someone had just turned on a movie, a vision of a radiant Presley carrying a child—his child —flashed in Kade's brain. The mental image stole his breath as he nodded and stepped back to close the car door. Someday Presley would get married and have her husband's child. Kade was disturbed by the thought but not as disturbed by how much he wanted that guy to be him.

CHAPTER 7

PRESLEY

Presley felt sick to her stomach as the GPS declared their final destination was ten miles away. Kade had been really quiet for the past thirty minutes, making her feel worse. She was putting him in a really bad situation and felt selfish. It wasn't too late. They could always say she had nowhere to spend Christmas, and Kade felt sorry for her and invited her to be with his family. Or he could drop her off somewhere, and she could call for an Uber to take her back home.

"So," Kade said, letting out a big breath. "I need to tell you something."

Uh-oh. That didn't sound good. Maybe he was trying to think of a nice way to get out of this and that's why he'd been so quiet. "Okay." She placed a hand over her stomach, wishing she hadn't eaten so much candy. She avoided junk food when she was training, but Kade had come out of the convenience store with a bunch of treats, including two bags of chocolate covered cinnamon bears. "I'm listening."

Kade flicked his eyes at her before focusing on the road again. Then he drew in another deep breath. Presley couldn't stand to see him so stressed out. "We don't have to go through with this."

"What?" he asked, shooting her another quick look. "Are you getting cold feet already?"

"Isn't that what you have?"

"Not exactly."

"Then what's going on?" Presley asked although she wasn't sure she wanted an answer. "You've been very quiet, and I can't help but think you want out of this deal."

"No." He ticked his head to the side like he was cracking his neck. "Stacie knows we're engaged."

All the air in Presley's lungs whooshed out with a gasp. "You told her?" she choked out.

"You okay?" Kade asked, giving her a worried look.

"Fine." Presley wheezed in a breath, wondering if she was having a panic attack. "Just give me a sec to catch my breath."

"Should I pull over in case you need mouth to mouth?"

Mouth to mouth? What was he trying to do? Kill her? "No mouth to mouth!" she said a little too loudly. Embarrassed by her outburst, she gently cleared her throat. "Really, Kade. I'm fine."

His lips twitched, and she could tell he was on the verge of laughing. Thinking of his mouth pressed to hers made her realize they had yet to discuss what level of intimacy they planned on having while engaged. "By the way, I'm not sleeping with you."

"What?" Kade jerked his head and looked at her, making the car swerve. He quickly straightened the wheel out and then shot her another look she couldn't quite decipher. He appeared angry while at the same time flustered. "Where did that come from?"

"I meant, we aren't sharing a bed. Or a room."

"Yeah, I planned on sleeping separately." His fingers curled around the steering wheel so tightly his knuckles blanched. "Again, where did that come from?"

How did she explain herself without sounding like even more of an idiot? "When you said mouth-to-mouth, it made me think about kissing, and then I realized that we hadn't talked about kissing or, um, other stuff."

"Other stuff?" he asked with amusement.

Presley plucked a chocolate covered cinnamon bear out of the bag Kade had opened and threw one at him.

"Hey," he said with a laugh. "Driving here."

"Just forget what I said." She wanted to chuck another cinnamon bear at him when his grin widened. She refrained since it had started snowing about an hour ago and was now sticking to the road. As irritated as she felt, she didn't want to cause an accident.

He glanced over at her and grinned. "You're cute when you're mad."

Presley's stomach dipped at the wicked grin on his face. Did he know what that kind of talk did to a girl? He winked, letting her know he was perfectly aware his flirtatious comments were making her all hot and bothered. Narrowing her eyes, she threw another cinnamon bear at him. It hit him on the side of his head. "Bullseye," she said with a wicked grin of her own.

"Would you stop throwing things at me?" He slowed the vehicle down and glanced over his right shoulder before merging into the far right lane. "We need to get back on topic."

Oh, yeah. He was about to tell her something important. "Okay, so you told Stacie we're engaged. Why exactly did you do that?"

"I think I better pull over just to be safe." He eased the SUV off the road to a wide space for emergency vehicles and put on his flashers. Presley's insides swirled like her Vitamix when he turned to face her. "I told Stacie about the engagement after she told me my mother invited my ex-girlfriend to spend Christmas with our family."

The contents of Presley's stomach threatened to spew out of her mouth as the blood drained from her head.

"Take a deep breath," Kade said, flipping the temperature of the heater to cold. "Do you need an emesis bag?" he asked, turning the vent toward her face as fresh air blasted her.

"Why do I need an enema?" she asked, questioning his skills as a paramedic.

Kade's eyes widened before he burst out into raucous laughter. After a few seconds, he composed himself long enough to explain that emesis was another word for vomiting. She wondered how funny he thought it would be if she puked all over the front of his shirt.

"I'm not going to throw up." She tucked a loose curl behind her ear and adjusted the air vent, so it wasn't directly blowing in her face. "I was just shocked that your ex-girlfriend is going to be spending Christmas with us."

"Welcome to the club." Kade shoved a hand through his dark hair, leaving it rumpled and sexy. "That's not all." He paused, looking like he might need an emesis bag. "My mom and Jillian's mom have been best friends forever. They're actually more like sisters, and they also decided a long time ago that they want Jillian and me to get married."

Presley felt sick inside all over again. What was Kade trying to tell her? That he was still in love with this Jillian and now pretending to be engaged to her was going to screw it all up? Before she could ask him, he explained about Jillian's parents and why his mom had invited her to spend Christmas with their family. That made Presley feel a tiny bit better until he mentioned that his mom was determined that he and Jillian get back together.

"Is Stacie the only one who knows about me?"

"Yeah, but I can't guarantee she hasn't told my sisters yet." His brow furrowed, making her want to reach across and smooth her finger over the lines. "Why?" he asked with concern.

Presley didn't want to cause any problems. What if Kade's feelings had changed, and he wanted to get back together with his old girlfriend? He certainly couldn't do that with Presley hanging around.

"You don't have to go through with the engagement thing. I'll figure something else out." She let out a shaky breath. "Just drop me off somewhere, and I'll take an Uber home."

"No way," Kade said, the lines on his forehead deepening into a scowl. "I am not putting you in some stranger's car and sending you home to spend Christmas alone." Before she could come up with a valid argument, he added, "And I need to be engaged now more than ever."

He did? "You...you aren't interested in getting back together with Jillian?"

"No, she and I tried dating for a few months, but it wasn't right." The muscle in his jaw flexed. "Jillian agreed, and we parted as friends, but my mom and Jillian's mom are still holding out hope we'll get married."

And now he was pretending to be engaged to Presley, which was bound to cause all kinds of problems. If they were really engaged, then Presley could try to win his mom over. But they weren't engaged, and there was still a chance Kade might still have feelings for Jillian.

"I can tell what you're thinking, Presley, and you're wrong," Kade said. "I don't want to get back together with Jillian, but I don't want to hurt her either. My mom is dead set on me marrying her best friend's daughter. If I'm engaged, then Jillian won't get her hopes up."

"But we're not really engaged."

"Technically, we are because we both agreed to it."

Presley tried imagining what this Jillian looked like. She bet she was gorgeous and exactly Kade's type. She had to give him an out in case his feelings changed once he saw her again. "Will you promise me something?" Presley asked, biting her lower lip, so it didn't quiver.

"Depends on what it is."

"If you find that your feelings have changed for Jillian, then you need to tell me, and I'll end things between us."

"Presley…"

She held up her hand. "Promise me."

"Fine, I promise."

"Thank you."

"So, are we still engaged?" he asked, running a hand across his darkening whiskered jaw. Firefighters had to be clean-shaven so that their masks fit properly, but she'd noticed in the past that when Kade was off for more than a few days, he'd let his beard grow into a sexy five-o'clock shadow. Presley's fingers itched to caress that square jawline. Her eyes drifted to his mouth. Kade's lips were perfect, full but not in a feminine way. She'd bet her meager salary along with Brynlee's that Kade Hunter knew how to thoroughly kiss a woman, too.

Her gaze flickered up, and Presley nearly went into full cardiac arrest. Those silvery blue eyes of his were filled with a hunger that made her feel breathless again. She might not be too experienced when it came to men, but she was fairly certain Kade wanted to kiss her as much as she wanted to kiss him.

Her body swayed toward him. Just as Kade leaned toward her, a diesel flew past them, swirling up snow and making the windows of the car rattle. It was enough to snap both of them out of whatever the heck had just happened.

"All right," she said, holding out her hand. "The engagement is still on."

"Okay." A sinful smile spread across his face as Kade pressed his palm to hers. Instead of shaking on the deal, he brought her hand to his mouth and brushed his lips across her skin. Spirals of heat spread through her like an out of control fire as their gazes locked.

"Ready to go?" he asked, lowering her hand but not letting go. His thumb made a slow circle in the center of her palm.

"As ready as I'll ever be," she said in a breathless tone. Honestly, Presley was an elite athlete in top physical condition. She shouldn't feel like she'd run a marathon by simply holding Kade's hand.

The next ten minutes flew by far too quickly. She and Kade went over their story again, but still never addressed whether they were going to kiss or not. When he pulled in front of his stepdad's cabin, Presley snorted a laugh as she stared at the enormous house made from stone and logs. "That is not a cabin," she said with another laugh. "That is a freaking mansion."

"It's a cabin." Kade glanced at the structure and unclicked his seatbelt. "But now you know why we won't be shacking up."

"Um, we wouldn't be shacking up even if there weren't twenty rooms to choose from."

"Twelve," he said. "Thirteen, if you count the Murphy bed in the family room."

"It's so…"

"Over-the-top?"

"Gorgeous," Presley said, her eyes skimming over the entire house. Single candles with flickering bulbs were in each windowsill. A lighted garland draped across the large porch with red bows at each post. A tall Christmas tree stood in front of a picture window, the colored lights muted by the glass. "It looks like one of the houses in Brynlee's Christmas village."

"My mom has one of those too. It takes her a month to set up."

"I can't wait to see it." Presley had always wanted a lighted Christmas village but never had the money. Even when they were priced at seventy-five percent off during the after-Christmas sales, it was a frivolous cost she couldn't afford. Brynlee's village was small with only a few houses, but it was still magical to look at. Someday Presley would buy her own village. Maybe if she won the *Ninja Champions,* that would be her first purchase. She wouldn't even have to wait for a sale.

"I might need an emesis bag," she said after Kade opened her door and helped her out. "Are you sure you want me here?" Presley looked up at Kade when he didn't respond right away. She expected him to make a wisecrack about enemas or something. Instead, he was gazing at her with a simmering and intense look. Electricity swirled in the air around them, and every inch of her skin buzzed at his nearness.

"Wanting you isn't a problem for me," he said in a gruff voice.

Oh. What exactly was he saying? That he wanted her here or he *wanted* her?

"Uncle Kade!" a child's voice cried out just before a little boy plowed into them, hugging Kade's legs and pushing Presley away. Since when had they gotten so close?

"We'll finish this later," Kade said, his eyes a smoky gray.

Presley didn't have time to ask for further clarification as more children joined in the Uncle Kade hug fest going on. He was very popular with his nieces and nephews. Really adorable nieces and nephews with an equally handsome uncle. She bet Kade would make pretty babies too.

Presley didn't dwell on that thought too long. One of the adult's ended the ridiculously cute reunion between the uncle and his little entourage. Seriously, how was Presley supposed to resist completely falling for Kade?

"Kids," a woman hollered out. "It's freezing out here. Let Uncle Kade come inside."

"I get to hold his hand," a little girl with curly blonde hair said. Presley recognized her as Maddie, Stacie's four-year-old daughter.

While two little girls that looked exactly the same fought over his other hand, Presley glanced at the front porch to see the adults filing out of the house. Butterflies the size of hummingbirds flitted around inside her stomach as she scanned each face. She'd air-dropped Kade's family picture to her phone and had studied it on the drive up, memorizing names and faces and who belonged to who. Identifying all three of Kade's sisters was easy, but she had trouble pinpointing which man they were married to. Three guys were huddled together on the other side of the women, watching Kade and their children. Presley couldn't really see their faces because of the low lighting.

She quickly skimmed over the onlookers once more, trying to find Jillian Hastings. Presley had looked her up online and discovered she was right about her being pretty. Jillian was gorgeous with dark auburn hair and a body she enjoyed frequently displaying on social media. Presley should get some tips from Jillian on how to take a selfie. Zuri was always after Presley to post pictures of herself in workout clothes, which Jillian did nearly every day. Seriously, *every* day. In fact, Presley may not recognize the woman fully clothed.

Kade's mother and stepdad were the last to come out of the house. Marilyn looked stunning in a red silk jumpsuit with wide legs. Her dark hair was cut in a chic short bob with one side tucked behind her ear. Diamond earrings sparkled like the stars on a moonless night, making Presley feel frumpy in her distressed skinny jeans and a long-sleeved tee. Thankfully, Mrs. Miles wasn't looking at Presley. Her eyes were glued to her phone as she typed in a message.

"Let's get these little munchkins inside," Kade said. "I'll come get our luggage in a minute."

"Okay." Presley felt a small hand slip into hers. She looked down to see a little girl with big brown eyes and her auburn hair pulled back into a sleek ponytail. "You're Brooklyn, right?" Presley asked as they followed Kade to the porch steps.

"Yesth," she answered with a hint of a lisp. "Who are you?"

"I'd like to know the same thing," a woman said with just enough of a bite to her words to leave teeth marks.

CHAPTER 8

KADE

K ade heard the tone in his mother's voice and immediately knew this wasn't going to go smoothly. He wanted to reach for Presley's hand as a show of solidarity, but Maddie was hanging onto his left hand while Jenny and Laura gripped his other one.

He shifted his focus to Presley, hoping the sassy Princess Warrior was close by. Cowering to his mother would only make things worse. He probably should've prepped Presley better. Heck, he wasn't prepared himself. It was a little hard concentrating since his pretend fiancée was wreaking havoc with his body. Now that Big Brother wasn't watching over them, the underlying attraction he'd suppressed for Presley had exploded into an inferno. She was driving him crazy.

Presley licked her lips and glanced at him. Her face at least had some color to it, but she wasn't smiling. She actually looked terrified. It ticked him off. He wanted to call his mom out but didn't want to make Presley feel any more uncomfortable.

"Hey guys," Kade said, pausing at the base of the porch steps. He was grateful when Jenny and Laura let go of his hand and raced up the stairs to hug his stepdad. With his hand free, he was able to reach over and take Presley's hand. Her fingers felt like icicles as she gripped onto him like she was hanging onto a lifeline. "Mom, I think you remember meeting Presley Windsor a couple of years ago at the badge ceremony."

"Yes, of course." His mom's eyes flickered to Presley's face and then down and their joined hands and then back to him. "Kade, darling," she said, her voice polite and refined but still lacking any warmth, "you didn't tell us that you were bringing a guest home with you."

Kade felt Presley stiffen at his mom's slight. "Sorry, but I wanted it to be a surprise."

"It certainly is that," his brother-in-law Greg said dryly. He was pretty sure Stacie had told her husband about the engagement.

"A surprise?" his mom asked, blinking rapidly like one of her eyelash extensions had fallen into her eye. "What do you mean?"

Maddie let go of Kade's hand and darted up the stairs, holding her arms up to her father. The child must have a sixth sense that things were about to get tense. Greg bent down and picked his daughter up and then grimaced at Kade and mouthed, "Good luck."

Squeezing Presley's hand, Kade tugged her closer to his side. He wasn't sure how to break the news without starting World War 3. Movement caught his eye, and he saw Stacie quickly move to their mom's side.

"Mom," Stacie said, sliding her hand around their mother's arm. "Why don't we all go inside and let the kids finish watching their show." She sent an apologetic look at Kade and Presley. "Then Kade can share his news."

"News?" his mom asked. "What news?"

"Sweetheart," Ben said, putting his arm around his wife's shoulder. "It's cold outside and rude to keep Kade and Presley standing in the snow."

Hearing the word *rude* snapped his mother into hostess mode. "Of course," she said, forcing her mouth up into a smile as fake as his engagement was to Presley. "Kade, please bring your guest inside." She spun around and took three-year-old Blake by the hand, leading him back into the house.

"Thank you," Kade said to Stacie. She nodded, and then helped Greg, Devon and Cody herd the other children inside.

"Kade," Jamie whispered, looking over her shoulder and then back at him. "I need to warn you that mom has a surprise for you too."

Allison moved in close to Jamie. "Yeah, we should've said something earlier."

"It's okay," he said, grateful his sisters were sensitive to Presley's feelings. "Stacie called an hour ago."

"So you know about…" Allison's words trailed off when their mother appeared at the doorway. "…the talent show, right?" she finished without hardly missing a beat.

"Yep, Presley and I are planning on it." He heard Presley inhale sharply, so he gently squeezed her hand to ward off another panic attack and to keep her from bolting on him. "Can't wait."

"What talent show?" Presley hissed as they mounted the porch steps. "And where is you-know-who?"

"We'll talk about it later," he said from the side of his mouth. And he had no clue where Jillian was, which he told Presley before crossing the threshold.

The house smelled like gingerbread. His mother and sisters baked it fresh every year for the annual gingerbread house contest. It was a fun tradition, and he was excited to share it with Presley. It kind of surprised him how much he wanted to share everything with her. He knew from being so close to Travis that their Christmas celebrations were far different from his. At least the Christmas's once his mother married Ben. In the blink of an eye, his mom had gone from an impoverished twenty-one-year-old widow to a billionaire's wife. The money hadn't affected Kade like it had his mother. Sometimes he wondered if she even remembered their former life.

"This house is amazing," Presley said, letting go of his hand to take off her shoes.

"It is beautiful," Kade said, glancing toward the great room where his family was gathering. "Hey," he said, waiting for Presley to meet his eyes. "I'm sorry about all of that out there."

Her blue eyes glittered with moisture, and she bit down on her lower lip. "Your mom hates me."

"She doesn't hate you."

"I'm not stupid," Presley said.

Murmurs from the other room drifted on the spicy scented air. It was clear a pretty intense conversation was going on with his family.

"I can still leave," Presley whispered in a shaky voice. "They still don't know anything."

Kade hated how wounded she looked. He'd promised Travis he'd protect his sister, and so far, he was doing a lousy job. He could handle his mom. He'd grown thick skin over the years. But how fair was it to subject someone as sweet as Presley to his mother and Jillian together? As much as he was enjoying the role of Presley's boyfriend, he needed to give her an out if she really wanted it.

"I don't want you to leave," he said, surprised by how much he really meant it. Something was happening between them. Something he hadn't counted on, and it wasn't just the sizzling chemistry that had surfaced. They were friends. She made him laugh, and he loved making her laugh. "But I will take you home this second if that's what you really want."

Presley considered him for a long moment, and he was afraid she might take him up on the offer. "I don't want to ruin your family's Christmas."

"You won't."

"What about your mom?"

"She'll come around once she sees how much … how great we are together," Kade said, stumbling on his words. He'd almost said how much I love you. *Love?* He didn't love her. He liked her. A lot. And he was attracted to her, but that didn't mean he was ready for this to all be real.

She studied him thoughtfully for several heartbeats before a small smile emerged. "I want to stay."

A stupid grin spread across his face. "There's my Princess Warrior," he said, not caring how sappy he sounded. Hey, if he was going to play the part, he might as well go all in.

"That makes you Prince Charming by default." Her lips curved up, the smile reaching her eyes. "You are kind of charming, you know."

"Yeah?" Kade teased back. He held out his hand and felt a rush of electricity surge through his veins when their palms met. "Okay, it's showtime."

"Right." The smile on Presley's face faltered. "This is all for show."

He hadn't meant it that way. Not really, but he didn't get a chance to say anything as Presley pulled on his hand, leading him into the lion's den. His family stopped talking as if someone had pulled the plug on the television. Kade still didn't see Jillian, which was a little disturbing. Where was she?

"Your home is beautiful," Presley said, addressing his mom and stepdad.

"Thank you," Ben said. "I hope you feel welcome here."

Again, Ben's hospitality prodded his mother to speak. "Yes, Presley, it's so nice to have you here." She gently cleared her throat. "Would either of you like anything to drink?"

"No, thank you," Presley and Kade answered in unison. They looked at each other and laughed. "We're good," Kade said.

The sick look was back on his mother's face. If she didn't have Botox, he was certain she would be frowning right now.

"Enough chit-chat," Stacie said, her pregnancy hormone voice coming off as demanding. Kade should've given his sister the other bag of chocolate covered cinnamon bears to make sure she remained calm. "I think you have something to share with us."

"Yes," his mother said. "We're waiting on bated breath."

His mouth suddenly dry, Kade swallowed and looked at his sisters and their spouses. Stacie and Greg were the only ones who looked pensive, which he assumed meant Jamie and Allie were still in the dark.

"Say something," Stacie mouthed.

"Right. Okay." Kade's palms felt slick, and he hoped Presley didn't notice. "Presley and I are engaged."

Kade had no idea who said what as the room erupted with raised voices. He only picked up on a few keywords, but it was enough to know that no one had expected his announcement.

"Engaged?"

"What?"

"Congratulations!"

"Are you serious?"

"Bro," Greg said, coming across the room with a grin on his face. "Congrats, man." He hugged Kade and then turned to embrace Presley. "Welcome to the family," he said, his voice barely heard over the cacophony of voices. "And, yes, it's always this crazy."

"Thank you," Presley said, looking like someone had zapped her with a stun gun. At least she didn't look as shell-shocked as his mother. Kade wondered if he should get his mom's vital signs just to make sure she was okay.

Stacie moved in front, blocking the vision of their mom. "I'm so excited my big brother is getting married!"

Jamie and Allie were right behind Stacie. They were genuinely excited, making Kade feel bad that it wasn't true. In theory, pretending to be engaged was supposed to help someone he cared about. He hadn't counted on the reality that his family would be happy for him or how disappointed they all would be when he and Presley broke up.

That thought made his chest feel tight like he'd entered a smoke-filled room without his protective mask on. It was weird that thinking about breaking off the engagement felt more like a trap than getting married.

He looked at Presley, watching her with pride as Jamie and Devon gave her a welcoming hug. A glow radiated from Presley's face, lighting up the room like the star on top of the Christmas tree. She was breathtakingly beautiful.

As if sensing him watching her, their eyes connected, and a hint of a smile lifted the corners of her mouth. "Hi," she said in a soft voice.

"Hi." His eyes skimmed over her pretty face, dipping briefly to her full lips. Man, he wanted to kiss her. But that would have to come later when things weren't so crazy. The grandchildren had abandoned their Christmas show to see what was going on with the adults. "You doing okay?" he asked when his nephew Lucas zipped past Presley, knocking her slightly off balance.

"Yes." Her gaze flickered to his mother, who was whispering to Ben. Their body language indicated the conversation was intense. Sighing, Presley looked back at him. "Is there a bathroom close by?"

"Yeah," he said, pointing his finger in the right direction. "It's just down the hall, first door on the left."

"Thanks," she said, slipping past him close enough to catch a whiff of her tantalizing scent. "I'll be right back."

Kade hoped so. He wouldn't blame her if she snuck out of the house and ditched him and his very loud family.

Allie stepped next to him, watching with him as Presley made her way down the hall. As soon as she disappeared into the bathroom, she nudged Kade in the arm. "Way to shake up the family party."

"You're welcome."

She grinned. "So, the Princess Warrior, huh?"

"Crazy, right?"

"So crazy," Jamie said, joining in on the conversation. "Mother isn't very happy with you right now," she said as if Kade wasn't already aware of his mother's displeasure.

"Thanks, Captain Obvious," he said dryly.

"Hey, don't leave me out of this," Stacie said, joining the circle. "What did I miss?"

"Mom isn't very happy with me," Kade deadpanned.

"No duh," Stacie said.

Kade smirked at his sister before looking over Stacie's head to see his mom furiously texting on her phone. He was pretty sure the recipient was Jillian.

"It's going to get worse once Jillian gets here, which could be anytime now," Stacie added, answering Kade's next question before he asked it. "She was supposed to be here hours ago but got stuck at work."

"Yeah," Jamie said, "I thought the latest plan was for her to come in the morning, but I'll bet you a hundred bucks she shows up tonight." She held out her hand for Kade to shake on it.

"I'm not betting against you," Kade said with a laugh. "I'm sure you're right."

"So," Allie said, leaning in closer, "have you guys set a wedding date?"

"Not yet." Kade rubbed a hand behind his neck. All of this was giving him a headache. "We're not in a rush."

"Good," his mother said, coming to stand behind her daughters. "That means it's not too late."

"Not too late for what?" Kade asked, noticing his sisters had abandoned him, scattering like candy from a broken piñata and leaving him to face their matriarch alone.

"To know if Presley Windsor is really the best option for you." She placed a hand on Kade's arm, concern, and a tiny bit of desperation lighting her eyes. "She's a lovely girl, Kade, but this all seems so rushed."

She had no idea how rushed, and she never would. "Mom, you haven't been very nice to her. What's up with that anyway?"

A flicker of remorse crossed his mother's pretty features. She'd just turned forty-seven, but still looked at least a decade younger. "I'm sorry, it's just I had someone else in mind for you."

"Let me guess," he said, casting a furtive look over his shoulder to see if Presley was still in the bathroom. "Jillian Hastings?"

"Who told you?" she asked, looking at each of her daughters with suspicion.

"No one needed to tell me anything," Kade said, not wanting to get his sisters in trouble. "Come on, Mom, you and Mrs. Hastings have pushed Jillian and me together for as long as I can remember."

"Well, that's because you all are perfect for each other."

"We already tried, and it didn't work out," Kade said.

"That was a long time ago. You haven't seen her for two years, and she is so beautiful and talented and fits into our family perfectly." She clasped her hands in front of her as if she was going to start begging him. "Olivia and I would get to share grandchildren. How perfect is that?"

"Mother," Kade growled irritably. "Please stop pushing Jillian on me. She and I both agreed that we're better off as friends."

"Well, if we're friends, you haven't been a very good one," a familiar voice said from directly behind him.

Kade didn't need to turn around to know that husky voice belonged to Jillian Hastings. Still, he turned to greet her and was surprised when Jillian quickly closed the distance between them. He caught sight of Presley coming down the hall just as Jillian kissed him soundly on the mouth.

CHAPTER 9

PRESLEY

Presley stared at her fiancé, lip-locked with the dark-haired beauty. A fierce possessiveness filled every part of her, while at the same time, she wanted to start crying. Kade was hers. At least for the next few weeks. This interloper had no right to lay one on her boyfriend.

"Whoa," Kade said, pushing the woman away from him. "What the heck, Jillian?" he asked, taking another step backward.

"My goodness, Kade," Jillian said with a light laugh. "It's not like we haven't kissed before." She tipped her head back and pointed to the greenery hanging from one of the beams. "Besides, we're under mistletoe, so we had to kiss. It's tradition."

Ah, so this was Jillian. She was fully clothed so that's why Presley didn't recognize her right away.

Kade looked up at the mistletoe and then settled his gaze on Presley. "Hey, I want you to meet someone," he said, making a wide arc around Jillian to reach Presley's side.

Jillian whirled around, her chocolate colored eyes tracking Kade as he took Presley's hand and made the introductions.

"Jillian, I'd like you to meet my fiancée, Presley Windsor."

"Fiancée?" Jillian asked as two perfectly sculpted eyebrows shot up with disbelief. "Why, Kade, I had no idea, or I wouldn't have kissed you like that."

Presley tamped down the urge to laugh out loud because this girl was fully aware of the situation thanks to modern technology and her ally, Marilyn Miles. "Hello," Presley said, wondering what the etiquette was on meeting an ex-girlfriend. She better not have to hug her. She was liable to squeeze too hard and make her pass out. "It's nice to meet you," she said, deciding it was better not to initiate any contact at this time.

Jillian didn't speak for several awkward moments as she scanned the length of Presley, starting from the top of her head all the way down to her stocking feet. Presley felt stupid while this girl blatantly sized her up. It didn't help that Kade's mother, sisters, and their spouses had formed a semi-circle around them, watching with rapt attention. Mr. Miles was playing it smart and had herded the grandkids back into the family room to finish watching the movie.

"You look so familiar to me," Jillian finally said in a low, raspy voice that was probably sexy to most men, including Kade. "What did you say your name is again?"

"Presley Windsor," Kade interjected. "Or maybe you know her as the Princess Warrior from *American Ninja Champions*?"

"No," Jillian said, tapping a finger against her lower lip. "That doesn't sound familiar. But then I'm not a *Ninja Champion* fan, either."

Good. Presley wasn't exactly a fan of ex-girlfriends, especially the conniving kind.

"I'm a fan," Stacie chimed in. "Presley was amazing last season when she beat out Poison Ivy."

Presley shot Stacie an appreciative smile. Kade's sister had clearly taken a side. She made a mental note to get her another bag of chocolate covered cinnamon bears the next time she and Kade went out.

"Yeah," Cody said. "Too bad you got knocked out of the next tier."

Devon and Greg both started talking about that episode while their wives stayed quiet. They were either remaining neutral or siding with their mother.

"So what happened?" Greg asked. "It looked like you had a hold of the ledge and then you fell."

"I know," Presley said, shaking her head. "It surprised me too, but looking back, I could see I landed at a bad angle."

The men asked a few more questions as if Kade's ex-girlfriend wasn't standing there glaring at her. "Are you ready for the new season?" Devon asked.

"Yeah," Kade answered for her. "In fact, Presley has been chosen by the network to be on their season kick-off New Year's special." He squeezed her hand and addressed his mother. "Mom, we haven't had a chance to talk to you, but the network is sending out a camera crew to the cabin to film me proposing to Presley."

"We're going to be on television?" Marilyn asked, sounding excited for the first time since Presley and Kade had arrived.

"Wait a minute," Jillian said. "Are you saying that you haven't actually asked her to marry you?"

"Of course he's asked her," Stacie said. "They're only doing it for the viewers."

"When are they coming?" Marilyn asked. "There's so much to do, and I have no idea what to wear."

"Mother," Stacie said. "They're coming to film Presley and Kade, not our family."

Disappointment dulled Marilyn's eyes. Presley knew this was her only chance to get on Marilyn's good side. She wasn't about to let this opportunity slip by her. "I'm sure they'll want to get footage of Kade's family. I can ask my agent about it tonight."

For the first time, Marilyn offered a genuine smile at Presley. "How kind of you, dear," she said in a voice that was far different from the tone she'd used earlier.

"That is kind," Jillian said, sidling up to Kade's mom and winding her arm through hers. "I'm sure you'll look stunning on camera, Marilyn. Are you using a new cream because I swear you look ten years younger."

Jillian's flattery was enough to remind Marilyn whose side she was on. "Thank you, sweetheart," Marilyn said, giving Jillian a quick hug. "My dermatologist created her own skincare line, and it is simply a miracle worker."

"Suck up," Stacie murmured just loud enough for only Presley to hear.

Presley really wanted to hug Stacie, but Jillian was moving in with a predatory gleam in her eyes. "I'm dying to see your ring," she said, reaching out and grabbing Presley's left hand. "Oh," she said, not feigning how unimpressed she was. "How lovely."

Presley wanted to snatch her hand away but the rest of the women had all moved in to get a good look at the ring.

Kade's sisters were kinder, pointing out different things like how delicate the setting was and how good the white gold looked with Presley's skin tone.

"Kade," Marilyn said when it was her turn to look at the diamond ring, "that's not Grandma Hunter's ring."

Presley felt Kade's body go rigid. She had no idea what the significance was about his grandmother's ring, but one look at him told her he was upset. He visibly swallowed and licked his lips.

"It's my mother's wedding ring," Presley said truthfully. "She passed away when I was young, and I asked Kade if he was okay with me wearing her ring."

"That is very sweet," Marilyn said with unexpected tenderness. "And I'm so sorry for your loss."

"Thank you." Tears stung the back of Presley's eyes, and her throat felt thick as if she'd stuck a spoonful of peanut butter in her mouth. It was silly to want to win Kade's mother over. After all, she wasn't really marrying her son.

"That is sweet," Allison said just as one of the kids started crying from the other room.

"That sounds like Blake," Jamie said, glancing at her watch. "It's almost bedtime for him. Once I put him down, we can start the gingerbread house competition."

"I just love that tradition," Jillian said as Jamie and her husband went to get their son. "Kade, remember when we collaborated and made the two-story house that won the grand prize?"

Presley could tell Kade was still recovering from the Grandma Hunter ring comment and didn't answer Jillian. His mother, on the other hand, jumped right in and continued reminiscing.

"I remember that house," Marilyn said as Ben came into the room carrying Stacie's daughter. She was sound asleep on her grandpa's shoulder. "I have a picture of it in the Christmas photo album. We'll have to look at it later."

Jealousy sliced through Presley like a newly sharpened knife, cutting her deeply. She didn't have the kind of history Jillian had with this family. The Christmas photo album would be filled with photos of Jillian and Kade over the past years.

"Let me take her, Dad," Greg said, transferring the sleeping angel from his father-in-law to his arms.

The other children had migrated back into the room. Kade let go of Presley's hand to pick up Brooklyn. Marilyn directed the older children toward the kitchen with the promise of a snack, and Ben went with his wife. Allie held out her arms for Brooklyn, but the little girl shook her head. "I want Uncle Kade to carry me."

"Be right back," Kade said before following his sister to the kitchen, leaving Presley with Cody and Jillian.

"Sorry, ladies," Cody said with a smile. "I need a snack too."

That left Presley all alone with Jillian. Before she could come up with an excuse to find Kade, Jillian plastered on a smile. "Well, it's just us girls."

"Yep."

"I'm anxious to hear how you and Kade met each other." Jillian must like invading people's personal space. She wound her arm through Presley's like they were besties catching up. "So, how long have you known Kade?"

"For the past seven years," Presley said, eyeing the path to the kitchen. What was taking Kade so long?

"Really?" Jillian arched a questioning brow. "I don't recall him ever mentioning your name," she said in an overly sweet voice.

"I don't recall him mentioning you, either," Presley said just as sweetly.

The corner of Jillian's eyes twitched as her smile widened, revealing perfectly straight teeth. "Have you and Kade set a wedding date?" Her voice was as tight as a piano string.

"Not yet." Presley's gaze darted toward the kitchen. Where in the heck was Kade? "We're not in any hurry."

"Well, I guess that means you aren't pregnant," Jillian said with a tinkling laugh that was as fake as her boobs.

"Hey," Kade said, rescuing Jillian from getting her eyes scratched out. Presley had never understood that term until now. "Let's go get our luggage, and I'll show you to your room."

Presley was a breath away from declaring she and Kade would be sharing a room but kept her mouth shut. No need to get any further on Marilyn's bad side. While she was getting settled, Presley would have to brush up on her flattery skills. It seemed to be one of the only ways to get Kade's mother to smile.

"I'll come with you," Jillian said as if being the third wheel wasn't awkward or anything. "I need to get my stuff too."

The trip outside was as uncomfortable as a poorly fitted bra. Presley chafed at Jillian's happy chatter, but Kade bought right into it, laughing at the cute little stories Jillian had in her arsenal. Like the time they teamed up for the annual Christmas talent show and sang a duet. Presley had no idea Kade could sing. She wondered what else she didn't know about this man she was pretending to be engaged to.

By the time they made it to their perspective rooms, Presley was ready to shove Kade out her window. Didn't he see what Jillian was doing?

"Kade, do you mind if I take this room?" Jillian asked when Kade set his bag by the door of the room next to Presley's. "I don't mind sharing the bathroom with Presley, and then you can have a bathroom all to yourself."

"Uh, sure," Kade said, picking up his duffel. He glanced at Presley. "I'll just be on the other side."

"Sounds good," Presley said, forcing her lips into a cheesy smile, so she didn't stick her tongue out at Jillian. "I'm going to change, and then I'll meet you downstairs."

Kade's dark eyebrows bunched together. Presley needed to cool down before she said or did something stupid. She slipped inside her room and firmly closed the door before Kade had a chance to say anything.

Her anger was temporarily disabled as she took a good look at her luxurious accommodations. Most people only decorated one or two rooms for Christmas, but Marilyn was not most people. The entire room was tastefully adorned with beautiful

Christmas décor of silver, white, and red. There was even a small Christmas tree in the corner with red and white twinkling lights and mini glass ornaments. The best part was the Christmas village on top of the dresser.

Presley skimmed her palm over the handmade Christmas quilt covering the queen-sized bed as she crossed the room to look more closely at the miniature houses. There were only four but each one had a magical Christmas scene depicted in the window, backlit by a small light. Presley wished she could shrink down and go into each house.

A clanking noise sounded through the door of the Jack and Jill bathroom connected to the room next door. Irritation at Jillian put a damper on Presley's cheerful mood like someone had snuffed out a candle. She wanted to throw something at the door when Jillian started singing a lovely rendition of "I'm Dreaming of a White Christmas" while she showered. Her crystal clear voice floated on the air and drifted inside Presley's room through the crack underneath the door.

The immature side of her wanted to roll up a towel to close off the gap. She was searching for a towel when her phone pinged an incoming text.

Thinking it might be Kade, she ignored the message for all of twenty seconds. Digging her phone from her front pocket, she saw Brynlee's name on the screen.

Brynlee: *Just checking in with you to see how it's going.*

Presley: *Kade's mother doesn't like me, and his ex-girlfriend showed up and is staying in the room next to mine.*

. . .

Brynlee's reply was a video call. Presley didn't want to be overheard, so she opened the closet doors and climbed inside before answering the phone.

"Shut up," Brynlee said, her eyes wide with shock. "I didn't even know Kade had an ex-girlfriend."

"Well, he does," Presley said, leaning back against the closet wall. "Her name's Jillian Hastings. Oh, and get this. Not only is she his ex, but she's also a close family friend and BFF's with Kade's mom."

"No way." Brynlee squinted at the camera. "Where are you?"

"In the closet." Presley turned her phone around to show Brynlee the room and the adjoining door to the bathroom. "Jillian and I are sharing a bathroom."

"Nice digs," Brynlee said when Presley turned the phone back around.

"I know." Presley wished she could take Brynlee on a virtual tour of the house but figured it would be too tacky for someone like Marilyn Miles. "This house is not a cabin. It has twelve bedrooms."

"Wow, the network is going to love filming there."

"They will." Presley wrinkled her nose. "I wonder if they'll do a nice little segment on my fiancé's ex-girlfriend spending Christmas with his family."

"Wait," Brynlee said. "Are you telling me she's staying for Christmas?"

"Uh-huh," Presley said, noticing that Jillian was now singing, "All I Want for Christmas is You." Ignoring the melodious voice, she told Brynlee everything, including the mistletoe kiss Jillian and Kade shared.

"Sounds like she's desperate." A mischievous glint danced in Brynlee's eyes. "Speaking of kissing...have you and Kade broken any rules yet?"

"No, but there were a couple of close calls where I thought Kade wanted to kiss me." Presley shook her head. "It was probably just my imagination."

"Girl, Kade has wanted you for a long time. Travis is too blind to see it, and you and Kade do a nice little dance around the sizzling chemistry as if ignoring it will make it go away."

Presley's heart skipped a couple of beats as she considered Brynlee's words. There were times over the past couple of years that she sensed Kade was attracted to her, but he never acted on it. "Maybe I should drag him underneath the mistletoe and kiss him as a test. If he responds, then I'll know he's into me."

"Do it!" Brynlee said. "Do it even if there isn't mistletoe. You all are engaged and are allowed to kiss."

"I should probably wait until we aren't surrounded by his family," Presley said. She smiled, thinking about Kade interacting with his sisters' children. "You should see Kade with his nieces and nephews." She launched into a narrative, describing each child and how cute Kade was with them.

"Oh, sweetie," Brynlee said. "I knew you liked Kade, but I didn't know you're in love with him."

Presley thought about denying it, but the way she felt about Kade was the one honest thing in this whole fake fiancé gig. "Ugh, unrequited love sucks," Presley said.

"I don't think it's as hopeless as that," Brynlee said softly. "Kade just needs to open his eyes."

The shower had stopped, but Presley's semi-roommate was singing "Baby It's Cold Outside." It was the song she and Kade sang together a few years earlier. Was Jillian practicing for an encore with Kade?

"Oh, I forgot to tell you that Jillian has spent many Christmas's here and participated in their annual family talent show." She went on to explain how Jillian and Kade sang a duet together. "Kade already told his sisters that we are planning on doing something for the talent show but I don't know what to do unless throat-punching Jillian counts as a talent."

"Not sure that would win over Mommy Dearest," Brynlee said with a snicker. "But I'm sure we can come up with something for you to do."

"Like what?"

"Well, you're an amazing athlete."

"Thanks, but I doubt they have an obstacle course nearby." Presley tapped the back of her head against the wall. "Seriously, I feel like Sandra Bullock's character in *Miss Congeniality*, trying to come up with a decent talent, only I don't have Michael Caine to help me."

"I'll be your Michael Caine and will think of a talent for you," Brynlee said. "That reminds me, have you unpacked yet?"

"Not yet," Presley said, knowing she needed to do it sooner than later, so her clothes didn't get too wrinkled. "What does that have to do with Michael Caine?"

"Nothing, but I remembered that I packed that little red dress for you just in case you need to go formal." Brynlee gave her an exaggerated wink. "Or need to dazzle Kade with a sexy dress."

Brynlee was the one who made Presley buy the little red dress, which Travis wasn't too keen on her wearing out in public. Her older brother was funny. Presley wore sports bras and shorts to workout in all the time, but according to him, the red dress showed off too much of her assets.

A knock on the door made Presley yelp. "I gotta go." Scooting out of the closet, she stood up and whispered, "I'll call you later."

"Kiss him," Brynlee said before Presley ended the video call.

"Yes?" Presley asked when another knock sounded on her door.

"Hey, it's Kade. Are you ready to head downstairs?"

"Not yet," Presley said, looking down at her clothing. She hated to wear another outfit just for making gingerbread houses. But she did want to brush her teeth and touch up her makeup. "Go ahead, and I'll be down in a few."

"You sure?" he asked, the tone of his voice sounding a little disappointed. "I can wait."

The sincere tone tugged at Presley's heart. She couldn't stay mad at him forever. Tucking her phone into her pocket, she crossed the hardwood floor and grasped the doorknob. Shaking off her nerves, she rolled her shoulders back and opened the door. Whatever cute or sassy thing she was going to say got stuck in her throat as she stared at the sexy man standing in front of her. Kade was freshly showered, wearing well-worn jeans and an off-white button-down shirt with the cuffs rolled. She inhaled sharply and caught the yummy scent of his soap and deodorant.

"What?" he asked when she continued staring. "Do I have something on my face?" He rubbed a hand across his whiskered jaw. "Or do I need to shave?"

"Don't shave," Presley said, curling her fingers into her palms so she didn't reach out and stroke his jawline. "I like it."

"Yeah?" Kade's blue eyes darkened as awareness arced between them like a live wire. His gaze drifted to her mouth and lingered there for several heartbeats. That hungry look was back in his eyes when he looked back up. Brynlee's demand that Presley kiss him echoed in her mind as she slanted forward.

"You two ready to go downstairs?" an irritating voice said, ruining the moment.

Kade let out a big breath and ran a hand through his dampened hair before looking over at Jillian. "Yeah, we were just about to head down."

His voice sounded husky and slightly irritated. Presley was feeling a tad annoyed as well. That was the third time they'd almost kissed and then been interrupted. It was like a clichéd scene from one of Brynlee's romance books. Presley was tempted to go ahead and kiss Kade anyway. But a first kiss shouldn't be rushed or have an audience. A first kiss should be slow and soft so the two people involved could explore and taste before deepening the kiss.

"Presley?" Kade asked, reaching out to touch her on the arm. "You doing okay?"

Startling at the touch, Presley nodded her head, hoping Kade wouldn't ask her why her face was flushed and her breath was ragged.

Holy cow, if just thinking about kissing Kade did this to her, what would happen when they actually did kiss? And they would kiss. Presley wasn't letting another opportunity pass by her. She was kissing Kade before the day was over.

"I'm fine." She could feel Jillian's cold glare and darted a quick look her way. Yep, Jillian's eyes were like chips of ice. "You look nice," Presley said as envy twined around her insides like a fast-growing vine twisted around the other plants to choke it out. Jillian had changed into a curve-hugging Christmas t-shirt she'd probably ordered from some cute shop on Etsy and paired it with black distressed skinny jeans with a raw hemline.

"Thank you," Jillian said with an evil smile. Okay, so it wasn't exactly evil, but that's what if felt like to Presley. "I designed it myself." Her eyes made a quick perusal over Presley. "You should check out my Etsy store."

"Maybe I will," Presley said, although there was no way she'd ever order one of Jillian's shirts. It would be like wearing a Poison Ivy shirt to the first competition of *American Ninja Champions*. Looking back at Kade, Presley pushed a loose strand of her hair behind her ear. "Let me change, and I'll be right down."

"You don't have to change," he said with an appreciative gleam in his eyes. "You look good."

Jillian made a tiny noise that sounded like she might be choking on her tongue. Score one for Presley.

"Thank you," she said, stepping out of her room and closing the door behind her. Then she did something brave and kissed Kade on his whiskered cheek. "You look good too," she said, feeling like she'd just made a three-pointer.

Because this game was on, and Presley never stepped away from a competition she didn't plan on winning.

CHAPTER 10

KADE

K ade pulled his phone from his pocket and took a few more pictures of Presley helping Brooklyn make her gingerbread house. It was sweet how she'd volunteered to let the little girl help her since she was too little to do it by herself. It freed up his sisters and their spouses to create their own masterpieces. His mom and Ben were the judges, and the prize was usually something nice. No one knew what it would be. Last year, it was a full day at a spa and a two-hundred-dollar gift card. The kids all won prizes, but the adults were in it to win it. Yeah, his family was slightly competitive, but it was a healthy competition. Mostly.

Presley glanced up and caught him watching her. It wasn't the first time, but he couldn't help watching her. She was gorgeous and as sweet as the frosting holding the gingerbread together. She smiled shyly, her cheeks turning a lovely shade of pink. "How's your house coming?" she asked from across the table.

"Meh," he said, looking at the fire station he'd started building. His mom had purchased several three-paneled cardboard displays that kids used for the science fair and cut them lengthwise for each person to hide their house behind until it was time to judge them. His wasn't too bad, but if he didn't stop staring at Presley and get to work, it wouldn't be done. "What about yours?"

"So cute, right?" she asked Brooklyn.

"Yesth," his niece answered. "It'sth pretty." Kade grinned. He loved the way Brooklyn talked. His mother was after Jamie to get her into a speech therapist, but Jamie wasn't too worried. Lucas had the same lisp and outgrew it before starting kindergarten.

Kade glanced at Jillian, wishing she wasn't acting so weird. They were friends. Or at least they had been friends, but the reminiscing was getting really old. At first, he'd thought it was just her way to make herself feel better since she'd been invited for Christmas with the express purpose of him being her Christmas present. But her claws were out, and she wasn't going down without a fight.

Her gaze flickered up and caught him watching her. She flashed a white-tooth smile his way and leaned toward him. "No cheating," she said in a flirtatious voice. It's not like he could see over the cardboard from his vantage point. "I'm going to win this year, and all without your help, thank you very much."

There she went again, reminding everyone present that they'd teamed up on more than one occasion.

"Sorry, Jillian," Stacie said. "This year it's all me, baby." That started a new debate over who was going to win. Stacie winked at him, letting him know she had done that on purpose.

Kade was grateful for Stacie. More outspoken, even without being pregnant, she'd sided with Team Presley. Greg, Devon, and Cody were huge *Ninja Champion* fans so they were also Team Presley, although not as obvious as Stacie. It was a no shock his mother was Team Jillian or that Ben was siding with his wife, but his mom wasn't entirely vexed with Kade and his new fiancée. He hoped his mom's softening was because Presley was winning her over and not that his mom was excited about being on television. Presley had confirmed with her agent that the network wanted the family to sign waivers because they may include footage of them all together.

His gaze shifted to Jamie and Allie. Both of them were still Switzerland. He got the feeling they really wanted to declare Presley as their pick but didn't like causing any waves with their mom.

"Fifteen minutes," Ben called out from the recliner in the other room. His mom and stepdad stayed in the family room, so they didn't see the houses until they were complete.

"Did you all get the time?" his mom said, sticking her head in the kitchen. She'd periodically looked in on them, mainly to see if the older grandkids needed help.

"Yes, ma'am," Cody answered. "You're gonna love mine, Mom," he added with a wink.

"Do not try charming me, young man," she said, wagging her finger in front of her. "You know it won't sway Ben or my decision."

Kade saw his mom take a peek at Brooklyn and Presley's creation. Her lips curved up as her gaze lingered on Presley and then her granddaughter. She quickly hid the smile when her attention shifted to Jillian. The two women held one another's gaze as if telecommunicating. Kade was kind of proud of his mom when she gave no indication that Jillian would receive preferential treatment. At least that's the way he'd interpreted the silent conversation.

Before finishing his gingerbread fire station, he met Presley's gaze one more time. She gave him a shy smile, shooting his heart rate to an unhealthy rhythm. He was dying to kiss her and needed to come up with a plan, so no one interrupted them again. Maybe they could sneak out and go hot tubbing tonight.

She broke eye contact with him when Brooklyn stood up and whispered something in her ear. Kade had to force himself to look away and finish his fire station. As he added the final touches, he couldn't help wondering what was going to happen when this was all over. He wasn't sure he and Presley could go back to their former relationship. Not when his feelings for her grew stronger and stronger with every passing second.

Ben called out five minutes, and everyone worked furiously to finish up. Kade's roof wasn't straight but the two garage doors looked pretty legit. When it was time, Ben and his mom came into the kitchen and ordered them to stop working.

While they explained the judging process and what they were looking for, Kade saw Jillian try to sneak a look over Presley's cardboard. Her eyes widened with either surprise at how good it was or how bad it was before she looked back at her construction. A prideful smile crept across her face, and Kade quickly averted his gaze before Jillian got the wrong idea. He hoped his design won on creativity rather than perfection. It would be fun to win the prize and then turn around and gift it to Presley for making the sacrifice to help his niece.

"All right," his mom said. "It's time to show us your houses."

Everyone removed the cardboard barriers, revealing a diverse collection of gingerbread houses. Brooklyn clapped her hands, excited for everyone to see the pink monstrosity she'd helped create. Everyone oohed and awed over it, even though it was clear Presley had let Brooklyn do whatever she wanted.

Jillian's house looked perfect. Almost too perfect when compared to the pink house Presley and Brooklyn made. Jillian was a graphic designer for multiple companies. She also had a lucrative online business, designing one-of-a-kind shirts, hats and aprons. Her gingerbread house reflected her flair for turning something simple into an elegant piece of artwork. She'd frosted the entire house with white frosting and then used silver sprinkles to cover the outside, so it sparkled like scattered diamonds under the lights. She'd embellished the edges, windows and door with gold and silver colored chocolate pearls.

Kade's fire station didn't win but it was a favorite with his nephew, Lucas. He gave it to the little boy with a promise to show him the new fire truck the next time his parents brought him for a visit. Jillian's house won a prize for the most beautiful, but the grand prize went to Greg. He'd created a bachelor's pad paradise complete with a large deck that featured a hot tub and a big screen TV he'd framed with pieces from a KitKat candy bar. The screen was white frosting with a football field drawn on it and stick figure football players he'd made with icing.

"Don't go inviting any single girls over to your bachelor pad," Stacie said, rubbing a hand across her baby bump. "I've watched enough crime television to know how to dispose of a body where nobody will ever find it."

"Duly noted," Greg said. Then he handed over his envelope containing a two-hundred and fifty dollar Visa gift card to his wife with the promise of a foot rub before bed. "My bachelor pad is yours, babe." Then he kissed Stacie soundly, earning a few groans from Jenny, Laura and Lucas.

Kade captured the moment on camera, wishing someone could get a picture of him kissing his fiancée. The hot tub idea was sounding better and better.

Kade was proud of his mom when she awarded Brooklyn and Presley prizes for the best pink gingerbread house. It was a new category his mother had made up just for them. "Smile," he said, taking several shots of his mom sandwiched between Presley and Brooklyn.

He started to get up to come over and congratulate the cute duo on their win when his mom handed Jillian her prize. "Kade, let's get a picture of our first-runner up." His mom slipped an arm around Jillian's shoulders and moved in close, so their faces almost touched.

"Say cheese," he said as he reluctantly framed Jillian and his mom's smiling faces on the camera screen. He wished Jillian had somewhere else to go for Christmas. Three was definitely a crowd.

Before the clean-up started, his mom announced that the talent show was the next evening. "We expect everyone to participate," she said, glancing at Presley when she said this. Kade felt bad at the look of terror on Presley's face. He always played the guitar and sang every year, usually with one of his sisters and a few times with Jillian. He planned on doing a solo unless Presley wanted to sing with him. "You're welcome to look in my craft room if you need any props."

The noise level rose a few decibels as they cleaned up the kitchen and dining room. Kade could tell his nephew and nieces were ready for bed. Laura completely lost it when the roof of her house caved in.

Jillian was busy chatting with his mother while they did the dishes together. They were laughing like they were best friends, with Jillian occasionally casting furtive glances at Presley as if to make sure she was paying attention to her.

Cranky kids and an ex-girlfriend trying to gain more of his mom's affection was getting to Kade. He wanted some alone time with Presley. So much had happened since their arrival. He wasn't sure if he needed to explain about his grandmother's ring or if he should wait and see if she brought it up. They also needed a game plan for when the camera crew showed up. Having Jillian here for the interview was awkward enough without having Presley's fans speculate about why his ex-girlfriend was with his family for Christmas. Maybe word wouldn't get out, but he wasn't counting on it. If the media could blow up a simple picture of Presley trying on wedding rings for her brother, then there was no telling what they'd do if they discovered he and Jillian had a past.

Catching Presley's eye, Kade smiled as he casually rounded the table and came up behind her. "Ready to get out of here?" he whispered in her ear.

"Yes," she said with a tiny shiver.

It was tempting to push her hair aside and place a kiss at the spot just below her ear. Instead, he took her hand and threaded their fingers together. With his sisters busy trying to calm their children down, Kade led Presley out of the kitchen and ran into Cody.

"Where are you two sneaking off to?" he said, wiggling his eyebrows up and down.

"Thanks, man," Kade murmured when all the attention was on them now. Then in a louder voice, he said, "I'm going to give Presley a tour of the house."

Jillian lasered him with the same look Stacie had given the bag of chocolate covered cinnamon bears. If Jillian asked to come along, Kade was going to lose it like his niece had over the broken gingerbread house.

"Will you peek in on Blake when you go downstairs?" Jamie asked as she tried calming down her upset daughter.

"Sure." Kade glanced at Stacie and Greg. "Want me to check on Maddie?"

"Yeah, thanks," Greg said.

Nodding, Kade and Presley turned to leave when Stacie stopped them. "Hey, Kade." She pointed to the beam above their heads. "Look at that," she said with a conspiratorial grin, "you two are under the mistletoe."

CHAPTER 11

PRESLEY

Tipping her head back, Presley saw the green sprig with red ribbon hanging above them. She hadn't noticed it there before and wondered who had moved it from the family room to here.

"Thanks for pointing it out," Kade said with a playful gleam in his eyes that made Presley's stomach swoop. "I guess we have to kiss," he said, sliding his hands up her arms and gripped her shoulders. "It's tradition."

He was teasing her and mimicking what Jillian had said to him right before she kissed him. Presley would've smiled if she wasn't freaking out inside. Sure, she was determined to kiss Kade before the night ended, but her fantasies had not involved an audience.

"We wouldn't want to go against tradition, right?" Kade asked.

"Yes." Her voice squeaked with the one-word answer that was wrong. "I mean no," she said with a nervous little giggle, which in turn made the others laugh.

Kade's lips edged up into a sexy grin that only intensified Presley's rapid pulse rate and messed with her breathing. She tried to relax while at the same time obsessed over kissing techniques. Of course, he might not even kiss her on the mouth. That made her feel a little more in control. "For tradition," she said, proud of herself for sounding so chill.

It was all fun and games until Kade tugged her closer and slowly lowered his head. Everything around Presley blurred when his mouth came down on hers soft and slow, lingering there with a tenderness that stole her breath. Her head spun as she kissed him back with an intensity that took her by surprise. Liquid heat swept through her, making her body feel weightless. She gripped the front of Kade's shirt, so she didn't melt into a puddle of pure bliss. Breathless, she gasped for air, but it came out more like a whimper. Her response was like an accelerant, fueling the already heated exchange as Kade increased the pressure on her mouth.

"Whoa, we better get the kids out of here before it gets PG-13," a voice said from far off.

"Oh my," another voice said, only it sounded like it was right next to Presley's ear.

As if someone had zapped her with a reality taser, Presley realized where she was and what she was doing in front of Kade's parents, siblings and ex-girlfriend. She ripped her mouth away when she remembered there was also children present.

Her breath uneven, Presley glanced around the room and wanted to disappear at the varying degrees of shock written on the spectator's faces. Well, they weren't the only ones shocked.

Presley was still trying to process what had just happened because that was one heck of a first kiss.

Daring to look at Kade, he wore an expression she wasn't sure how to interpret. Whatever it was, it had stunned him speechless. An awkward silence filled the room. Someone needed to say something.

"What a fun tradition," Presley said as if she and Kade had simply exchanged gifts instead of swapping DNA while kissing each other senseless.

"I'll say," Stacie said with a snicker.

Her snarky comeback made most everyone else laugh. All except for Marilyn and Jillian. Kade's mother looked confused, and Jillian looked determined.

"Okay," Kade said, snapping out of his trancelike state. "I'm going to give Presley a tour of the house now."

"Right," Greg said with a chuckle. "You two enjoy yourself."

"Just not too much," Stacie added with a wink. "Wouldn't want you getting on the naughty list with only a couple of days left until Christmas."

"Ha ha," Kade said, threading his fingers with Presley's. "We'll be back for hot cocoa and games."

"Don't forget to check on the kids," his sister called out as Kade led Presley out of the kitchen.

She heard a few more snarky comments about avoiding any more mistletoe as if Presley needed another reminder of that kiss. Oh boy, was she in trouble. Kissing Kade Hunter was unlike anything she'd ever experienced before. What's more, she wanted to do it again.

"So, um, that was interesting," she said once she and Kade were out of earshot of his family.

"Very," he said, leading her down the stairs to the lower level. "We probably need to talk about what just happened."

"Do we?" she asked, worried about what he might say. "We could just pretend like that never happened."

Kade stopped so abruptly, Presley nearly tripped over him. The serious look on his face was intimidating and kind of scary. "Pretend it never happened?" he asked as his heavy gaze dropped to her mouth, then slowly traveled back to her eyes. "That's not going to work for me."

Presley's skin felt tight, her throat and mouth suddenly dry. "No?" she asked, her voice coming out raspy and low.

"No," he said, walking her back until she was pressed against the wall. In a swift, hungry move, Kade kissed her with an explosion of passion that was completely consuming. Presley melted against him, letting her hands drift over the hard muscles of his chest. She gripped the front of his shirt again, this time to draw him closer. Her stomach felt bottomless as Kade eased the pressure on her mouth, giving her a series of slow, shivery kisses. His spicy warm scent flooded her senses and wrapped around her in a cocoon of pleasure that was making her brain fuzzy.

She made a small noise of protest when his lips drifted from her mouth, leaving a trail of heat as he migrated to place a kiss against her throat. Her knees threatened to buckle when his lips traveled back to her mouth to kiss her deeply, and she tightened her grip on his shirt. He tasted like chocolate and peppermint, a delicious combination that made her crave more.

Someone cleared their throat, ending the delicious kiss so abruptly it felt like Presley's oxygen supply was cut off. She sucked in a gulping breath and looked over Kade's shoulders to see his brother-in-law standing there with a grin. "Don't mind me," Greg said, barely holding back a laugh. "My wife needs her phone charger."

He passed by them and opened the door down the hall. Kade still had Presley backed up against the wall, glowering at his sister's husband. She should move, but his nearness was intoxicating, making her feel unsteady on her feet. She took in a shallow breath, catching the masculine scent of his cologne. She was tempted to bury her face in the hollow of his neck for a better whiff.

Greg came back out a second later, carrying a charging cord and battery power bank. "Carry on with that tour," he said, this time not holding back a deep chuckle.

"I plan on it," Kade mumbled. He returned his attention on Presley and started to move back but then he paused, allowing his eyes to drop to her lips. "Right after I finish what I started."

Lowering his mouth to hers, he took his time, kissing her long and slow as if this was the first time he'd kissed her and wanted to memorize the way her lips moved under his. Presley wasn't sure how long the kiss lasted, but Kade was the one to have enough sense to end it before they got caught again. "We have to stop," he said in a low voice that rumbled through her.

"Okay," she said, totally not committed as she pressed another lingering kiss on his lips.

"You're making me crazy," Kade said with a groan. His mouth descended on hers in a fast, hard kiss before he edged back to see her face. "Your brother is going to kill me."

"No he won't." She let go of his shirt and flattened her palms against his solid chest. She could feel his heart pounding in a rhythm that matched her own. "You're probably the only guy he trusts me to be with."

That was the wrong thing to say. "Oh man," he said, stepping back so her hands dropped to her side. "He trusted me, and I just broke every rule he gave me."

"First," Presley said, pointing a finger at him, "I'm a grown woman and don't need my brother telling me how I can or can't kiss someone." She narrowed her gaze when she saw humor flicker in Kade's blue eyes. "Second, his comments were more like guidelines rather than actual rules."

A small smile lifted the corner of Kade's mouth. "Are you quoting *Pirates of the Caribbean* to me?"

"Aye, mate," she said in a British accent and a whole lot of sass.

Kade laughed and pulled her into his chest, wrapping his arms around her. "I like the way you kiss," he said, pressing his lips to the top of her head. "A lot," he added, tightening his hold.

"I like the way you kiss too," she said with a contented sigh. She'd dreamed about a moment like this for so long that it almost didn't seem real. She never wanted it to end, which prompted her to ask a question she may not like the answer to. "What's going to happen to us when we go home?"

He stilled for a moment as if he needed to collect his thoughts. "I don't know." He set her back from him, sliding his palms down her arms to hold her hands. "We need to finish this week here and then decide what to do."

Anxiety took hold of her, its icy fingers squeezing her throat until she couldn't draw a breath. Maybe this wasn't as real as she'd believed. Maybe what had happened between them was all part of this fake relationship scheme. "Okay," she said, hoping he didn't notice the quiver of emotion in her voice.

A slight frown creased his brow as he tightened his grip on her hands, pinching her skin beneath her mother's wedding ring. It reminded her about his mother's comment concerning his grandmother's ring.

"Who is Grandma Hunter, and what ring was your mother talking about?"

Kade pulled in a hard breath and let go of her hands. "That was random," he said, sounding a little put out by the question.

"No it isn't," she said, feeling a little annoyed herself. "Your mother asked about it, and you looked like you needed an emesis bag." Or like he was about to get an enema, but she kept that part to herself.

"I was just surprised she remembered it," Kade said with a shrug.

"Really?" Presley asked, not buying what he was trying to sell to her.

Kade avoided looking her directly in the eyes and shifted on his feet as if contemplating if he should make a run for it. Presley should drop it, but she wanted to know now more than ever.

"Just before my grandma Hunter died a few years earlier, she gave me a diamond ring that belonged to her mother and her grandmother before that." He looked at her briefly before rubbing his thumb under his lower lip. "My mom knows that Grandma wanted me to give it my future bride."

Right, and Presley was only his pretend future bride. Now she felt stupid for pushing him. "That's really sweet." It also helped her to focus on the whole reason she was engaged to Kade in the first place. Just because they liked kissing each other didn't mean they were getting married. "Wearing my mom's ring makes me feel close to her."

A look of relief crossed Kade's features. Clearly, he was done with this conversation. "Ready to see the rest of the house?"

"Yes." She took his hand, knowing that it was highly unlikely there would be any more passionate kissing tonight.

Presley was awed by the large house. It even had a gym with free weights, a treadmill, elliptical, and a fancy cycle with a computer monitor to enhance the workout. She almost cried when Kade showed her the vast Christmas village his mother had set up in the large family room in the basement.

"Which is your favorite?" she asked Kade, already planning to sneak back downstairs sometime later so she could take it all in. "I think I like the yellow house with the couple dancing in the window."

"I've never thought about it," Kade said. "They all look the same."

"They do not," Presley argued. "Each one has a story. Wouldn't it be fun if you could shrink down and visit each house?"

When he didn't reply, Presley wondered if he'd ditched her.

She glanced up and found him watching her with the same expression someone had when they were trying to figure out where they knew a person from but couldn't recall. "You think I'm weird."

"Not weird." He cracked a lopsided grin. "I just never pegged you as the magical Christmas kind of girl."

"I love Christmas," she said, gazing back at the yellow house. The young couple dancing were dressed in old-fashioned clothes and looking at each other with so much love. She bet they were newlyweds and this was their first Christmas together. "It is magical."

Kade let her look a few minutes longer before he dragged her away to finish the tour with the craft room. Calling it a room was a joke. It was more like walking into a Hobby Lobby.

"Do I really have to do something for the talent show?" she asked, fingering a bolt of silky fabric. "Because I'm talentless."

Kade snorted a laugh. "You are extremely talented."

Presley noticed he looked at her mouth when he said this, but she wasn't about to go down that road again. "I don't sing, dance, or play the piano," she said. "I'm a *Ninja Champion* athlete, which comes from training and discipline, not talent." She held up her hand. "Even if it does take talent, it's not something I can do for your family's talent show."

He didn't argue with her but pressed her about her vocal abilities. "We can sing a simple Christmas song together, and I'll play the guitar."

"Kade, I'm serious when I say I don't sing." She remembered Jillian's gorgeous voice. "Are you and Jillian singing a duet again?"

Kade's eyes narrowed, and the muscle in his jaw ticked. "No, Jillian and I are not singing a duet together." He took a few steps forward until he stood in front of her. "I'm not interested in her like that," he said, looking all the world like he wanted to kiss Presley again.

As much as she yearned for his mouth to be on hers, she had to limit their physical contact, so she didn't fall for him more than she already had. "Maybe I'll be too sick for the talent show."

"That doesn't sound like the Princess Warrior. She would never walk away from a challenge."

He was right, but sometimes a girl had to do whatever it took to survive. And right now she had to move away from him. He was far too tempting to resist. Walking around, she looked in some of the bins on one side of the room. That's when she saw her answer for the talent show. The adults may not be impressed, but she knew the little kids would love it.

CHAPTER 12

KADE

Kade was anxious for the talent show this evening so he could find out what Presley was going to do. She wouldn't tell him, and it bothered him more than it should. He felt like she was shutting him out. Not that he blamed her. He'd totally screwed things up last night when she'd asked about his grandmother's ring. In his defense, his brain wasn't really fully functional. Her kisses were more potent than Kentucky bourbon and just as addicting. He avoided alcohol because he never wanted to be like his old man. He should've avoided kissing Presley too, but it was too late. He'd tasted her lips, and he was hooked.

Leaning against the doorjamb, he watched her as she played a board game with Lucas, Jenny, and Laura. Brooklyn sat on her lap, helping Presley again. The little girl had bonded with her, and Kade felt guilty because his sister Allison had commented on what a wonderful aunt Presley was going to be to her kids.

"Yes!" Lucas said, jumping up and down. "I win! I win!"

Presley laughed, the sound lighting Kade up inside like the town's Christmas light display. "Good job, buddy," she said, holding out her knuckles for a fist bump.

"That's not fair," Laura said. "It was my turn next."

"I know, sweetie," Presley said. "But you won the last game."

"I didn't win any games," Jenny said. "Can we play one more time, Presley?"

"Jenny, Presley might not want to play another round," Jamie said. She was knitting a baby blanket for Stacie. Kade noticed that Jamie was warming to Presley just like Allie.

"Let's play one more round," Presley said, smoothing her hand down Jenny's long hair. "Then it's time for lunch."

Kade was tempted to play the last round with them, but Jillian appeared at his side. "Hi," he said, wishing she wasn't standing so close to him. Jillian wasn't ready to concede to Presley and was determined to win him over. His mom hadn't conceded either, but more than once this morning, he'd seen approval in his mom's eyes as she observed Presley interacting with the family.

"Hello there." Jillian glanced at Presley and the kids, a slight frown creasing her brow. She was smiling again when she looked back at him. "I wanted to ask you a favor."

"What is it?" Kade asked, feeling like this was a setup.

"I was going to play the piano and sing for the talent show, but I think it will sound so much better with an acoustic guitar, and I wanted to know if you would accompany me?"

Jillian had come to his room late last night, asking if he wanted to sing a duet with her. Kade's answer wasn't what she'd wanted to hear, but she hadn't pressed him. He figured playing the guitar was okay and maybe a chance to set boundaries as friends.

"I'll understand if it will make your girlfriend feel threatened," Jillian said, running a finger lightly over his forearm. "She hasn't ever had a boyfriend before so she may not feel secure in your relationship."

"How do you know that?" Kade asked, moving his arm so she wasn't touching him anymore.

"Relax, it's all over social media." She smiled like she knew a secret. "I guess that's why her fans are so obsessed with knowing who this mystery Prince Charming is." Jillian held out her phone with the picture of Presley and Travis at the jewelry store. "Funny, that doesn't look like you."

Kade didn't comment on the photo since there wasn't much he could say. "Presley, and I have been friends long before it turned into anything else." He swallowed at the partial lie. It was getting harder and harder to separate what was real and what was part of the act. But the thing was that he'd been fighting his attraction to her for a while now. He had no idea how Travis would feel about him really dating his little sister. It was risky because if it didn't work out, then things could get weird between them, especially at the fire department where a good working relationship was critical.

"Kind of like us?" Jillian asked smugly.

He didn't want to engage in this conversation but needed to be clear about his feelings. At least with Jillian. His feelings for

Presley were still unfolding. "You and I are friends, Jillian. Only friends."

"I know that."

Blake toddled over to them and held up his arms. "Hold you," he said in that raspy little voice of his.

Kade was about to comply, but Jillian moved in and picked up the little boy. "Come see Aunty Jillian," she said as if that was supposed to change Kade's mind about her. He caught a whiff of a dirty diaper about the same time Jillian did. "Eww, gross," she said, making a retching sound that had Kade jumping back before she puked all over his bare feet.

"Take." Jillian retched. "Him." She retched again and held Blake out like she was about to drop him. "From me," she said retching several times in a row. It wasn't very flattering because every time she did it, her eyes kind of rolled back in her head.

"Come here, little guy," Kade said. As a first responder, he'd smelled a lot worse than this. "Let's get you changed, pal."

Blake's big brown eyes filled with tears. Kade wanted to cuddle him close, but he really was ripe.

"I've got him," Jamie said, taking her son and holding him close. It must be a mother thing, which impressed the heck out of Kade. "His tummy has been bothering him," she said, shooting a glare at Jillian who was holding her nose.

Kade patted the kid on the head, noticing a brown stain leaking through his pants. Jillian saw it too. Then she looked down and noticed some of the stain on the front of her white shirt. Kade swore her face turned green as she gagged and raced for the trash can, barely making it in time.

"Jillian, darling," his mom said, coming in just in time to see Jillian hurl into the trash can. "What can I do?"

Jillian couldn't answer. She was throwing up again. Kade felt bad and was pretty sure he had Zofran in his first-aid kit in the car. However, the anti-nausea medication wouldn't do much good if she couldn't hold anything down.

His mother kindly managed to get Jillian into the bathroom to shower while she went and got clean clothes for her. Jamie waited until they were gone before she told Kade that he would be stuck with dirty-diaper duty for the rest of his life if he married Jillian.

"You picked an amazing girl," Jamie added, nodding toward Presley, who was holding Brooklyn close and shielding her eyes from the unpleasant scene. "You better not screw this up," Jamie said in that don't-mess-with-your-sister voice before taking her son to change his diaper.

You better not screw this up. The words echoed through Kade's mind as he cleaned out the trash can. Apparently, Devon's stomach was as sensitive as Jillian's so Kade volunteered for the hazardous duty.

Presley and the kids had finished the game by the time he came back downstairs from taking a shower and changing into clean clothes. He knelt to help Presley put away the game since the kids had all ditched her.

"Where's an emesis bag when you need one, right?" she said with a tiny smirk.

"No kidding." He reached out for the dice at the same time Presley did and their fingers brushed. Electricity shot through him, and he froze as his eyes locked with hers. He hadn't touched her all morning. On purpose. Now he knew why.

"Whoops," she said, pulling her hand away from him. "I guess you've got those."

It took a few seconds for Kade's synapsis' to start firing again. She'd moved on to gathering the cards spread out across the floor. "You're good with kids," he said, hating the strain between them and knowing he was the cause of it.

"Thanks, but your nieces and nephews are so adorable."

"They are," he said, sliding a few of the cards closer to pick them up. "Even when they're stinky."

Presley bit down on her lower lip. He wished she wouldn't do that. It gave him all sorts of thoughts about tugging on that bottom lip before claiming her mouth fully. "We shouldn't make fun of her," she said, barely holding back a laugh.

"Yeah, that was brutal." He handed her his stack of cards, purposely letting his fingers remain in contact a tad longer than necessary. "But out of curiosity, how's your gag reflex when it comes to changing poopy diapers?"

She lost the battle to control her amusement and giggled. His stepdad came in to retrieve his iPad, and Presley reined in her mirth. Once Ben left, she nudged Kade in the arm. "I'll have you know I've done a lot of babysitting over the years and changed many dirty diapers." Her lips twisted into a wry grin. "I'm happy to report I never once tossed my cookies."

"I'm impressed," Kade said, handing her the last stack of cards. This time she was the one to let her touch linger, wreaking havoc with his sympathetic nervous system and bathing his brain with intoxicating feel-good chemicals. He totally got why Travis said and did stupid things because Kade asked Presley something he never thought he'd ever ask a woman. "So, do you want to have kids?"

Presley held perfectly still and stared at him for the span of a heartbeat. "With you?" she asked in a strangled voice.

Kade stifled a laugh, tempted to tell her that's exactly what he was asking. Before he could say anything, her face turned bright red. "Oh my gosh," she said, covering her cheeks with her hands. "You meant in general."

"Now you've got me curious." He shrugged and gave her a playful wink. "But for the record, I definitely want a few kids."

"Ah, did you hear that, Greg?" Stacie asked, making both Kade and Presley jump. "They're discussing kids."

"Yeah, one minute you're discussing having kids, and the next thing you know you're changing dirty diapers and puking in the garbage can."

"Greg," Stacie said, swatting him on the arm. "Do not say anything like that around Mother."

"What?" Greg smirked. "Devon almost lost it just hearing Jamie recount the story."

As if on cue, Kade's mom walked into the family room and stopped to look at them all through narrowed eyes. "Why do I get the feeling you all were just talking about me?"

"Now, Mom, you know you aren't supposed to ask any questions when it comes to Christmas."

Wow, that was smooth. Kade needed to take a few pointers from Greg on how to schmooze his mother.

A warm smile spread across his mother's lips. "You just might be my favorite son-in-law, but I'll deny it if you ever tell Cody or Devon."

"My lips are sealed," Greg said. "And I love you too."

His mom's gaze flickered to Presley. Remarkably, her smile didn't falter. "Presley, thank you for helping with the children."

A look of wonder crossed Presley's features, her blue eyes sparkling with emotion. "Thank you so much, Mrs. Miles."

His mother nodded her head, and just like that, her smile faded away. "Maybe we should postpone the talent show until tomorrow evening." She lifted her chin a notch as she met Kade's gaze. "Obviously, Jillian doesn't feel well."

"Obviously," Kade agreed in a slightly sarcastic tone that made the corner of his mom's eyes tighten with irritation.

"Does she need to be quarantined?" Stacie asked. "The last thing we need is for everyone to start dropping like flies."

"No, she doesn't need to be quarantined." Mom tucked a strand of her dark hair behind her ear. "She just needs some rest and maybe some chicken noodle soup."

"Maybe we should take the kids to see the new Christmas movie tonight," Stacie said. "That way Jillian can rest and the kids won't go stir crazy."

"That sounds fun," Kade said, loving the idea of not having Jillian breathing down his neck. "Presley, and I can come and help out with the kids."

Frustration flickered behind his mom's eyes. "Don't make any plans yet," she said in a strained voice. "Jillian might feel better.

Kade, perhaps you can look in on Jillian since you have medical training."

Kade resisted rolling his eyes. Jillian didn't need medical attention, but he supposed there was always a chance that she was coming down with something and that's why she'd reacted so strongly to the dirty diaper. "I've got Zofran in my first-aid kit," he said, noticing the way his mom's face lit up at the prospect of him spending some alone time with Jillian. "I'll get it before we go to the movie."

"What movie?" Allison asked, coming out from the kitchen. It was her turn to cook today, and she wore an apron covered with splattered spaghetti sauce. "I thought the talent show was tonight."

Stacie jumped in with the idea of taking the kids to the movies if Jillian was too sick for the talent show tonight. Allie didn't look quite as enthused. "Cody, and I already took Lucas and Brooklyn to it, and I'll be exhausted after cooking dinner for everyone too."

"That's okay," Stacie said. "Kade and Presley volunteered to go with us."

Jamie had come back upstairs and caught the end of the conversation. "Blake doesn't feel good, and I don't want to leave him with Devon. He's got a weaker stomach than Jillian."

"Jillian's stomach isn't weak," their mom said in fierce defense. "She doesn't feel well, either."

Jamie was still miffed over Jillian's treatment of her little boy. She looked like a mama bear about to take on another mama bear. Before things got ugly, Kade intervened. "Mom, why don't you go make some soup for Jillian." He placed his hands on his mom's shoulders and directed her toward the kitchen. "And I'll run out and get the medication."

"All right, thank you." His mom hesitated, and Greg turned back on his charm and escorted her to the kitchen with the promise to help her make the chicken soup.

"Oh brother," Stacie said, once they were out of earshot. "Have you two considered eloping?"

"No," Kade and Presley answered at the same time.

"Well," Stacie said, rubbing a hand over her stomach, "you should. Mom will start acting normal again, and Jillian will finally accept you are never going to marry her."

His sisters dispersed, Stacie promising to buy the movie tickets while Jamie and Allie rounded up the kids for lunch.

"Sorry my family is so crazy," Kade said when he and Presley were alone. "And I guess I should've asked if you wanted to go see the movie before I volunteered you."

"The movie sounds fun." Kade noticed she didn't say anything about his crazy family. She twisted her mom's wedding ring and looked toward the staircase. "I feel bad about making fun of Jillian if she's really sick."

Kade knew Presley was sincere and not just saying that to impress him or his mom. It was one more thing to like about her. "I'm sure she'll recover quickly." He could hear some of the kids coming up the stairs. "I better go get the Zofran for Jillian, and then I'll meet you in the dining room."

"Good luck," Presley said as Brooklyn ran to her and hugged her legs. "Call if you need backup."

"Thanks." Kade grinned and started walking backward, watching as Maddie made a beeline for Presley too. "Save me a seat."

"I'll try, but I'm kind of popular with your nieces and nephews." A sassy smile parted her lips as she patted the two girls on the head. "I think they like me better than you."

"What?" He shook his head even though it was probably true. Presley took time talking and playing with the kids and truly seemed to enjoy it. "I'm their favorite uncle."

"I never said you weren't." She blew him a kiss before taking Maddie and Brooklyn by the hand to help them wash up for lunch.

Kade stood there for a few seconds, unable to take his eyes off her. He loved watching her with his family. She was beautiful, kind, and fun to be around. Presley stopped at the end of the hallway and looked back over her shoulder, catching him watching her. Those perfect lips of hers curved into a sexy smile, sending his pulse rate into overdrive.

Presley had asked what they were going to do when they got home, and he'd given her a lame answer. But what *were* they going to when they returned home? Because Kade liked being with her. Liked her enough that if he wasn't careful, he could fall in love with her, and that thought scared him more than running into a burning building that was about to collapse.

CHAPTER 13

PRESLEY

Lunch was a noisy affair, but Presley loved every second of it. Especially since Jillian was still resting in her room. It was a welcome reprieve not to feel like she was in constant competition. Plus, it was nice not hearing any more cute stories about Kade and his ex-girlfriend.

The only drawback was feeling like Kade's mother was constantly taking Presley's measure. While she wasn't rude to Presley and had thanked her for entertaining the children, Marilyn still kept herself reserved and distant and always seemed to be watching her. Presley tried not to let it bother her and wondered if she would ever win the woman's approval. Then again, maybe it was better this way. It was hard to remember that this was all for show and that in two days, the camera crew would show up to film the proposal, and then once the special aired, she and Kade would end the charade.

Sneaking a look at Kade across the table, Presley bit back a smile as he demonstrated to his nephew Lucas how to properly slurp up his spaghetti noodles. Allison wasn't very thrilled that her brother was teaching this particular skill to her son, but she kept taking videos of them so she must not be too upset.

Kade met her eyes, giving her a smile that seemed reserved. She was confused about what was going on between them. Her feelings for him had only deepened, and her little crush was growing into something that felt an awful lot like love with every passing moment she spent with him. But he'd avoided being alone with her this morning so she'd reeled back in her emotions and pretended like she was only pretending to be in love with him. Playing with the kids was surprisingly fun as well as a great distraction.

Sensing Marilyn was watching her again, Presley averted her gaze and finished off the last of her salad. She avoided unnecessary carbs and pasta was one of those items. She'd much rather eat a cookie or a brownie, and Allison had made homemade brownies for tonight. Some people were weird about her meal prepping, but not Kade's sisters. They were so sweet about it and excited for the upcoming *Ninja Champion* season to start.

"Can we build a snowman yet?" Jenny asked her mother for the third time in the last five minutes. "Presley is done eating now." It had snowed during the night and finally let up an hour ago. The sun was shining, and the kids were anxious to go outside and play. None of the adults were too thrilled with the idea. But not Presley. She was just as excited as the kids were.

"Sweetie, Presley might not want to play in the snow." Jamie was holding a fussy Blake. The little boy sounded miserable.

"I can't wait to build a snowman," Presley said. "But I've never done it before so I'm going to need lots of help."

"I'll help!" Lucas said around a mouthful of spaghetti.

"Me too," Laura said.

"Can I come too?" Brooklyn asked.

"Sure," Presley said with a laugh. "But first, we need to help with the dishes." Presley stood up and picked up her plate.

"Oh no you don't," Allison said, scooting back from the table to start clearing the dishes. "If you're willing to play in the snow with the kids, then you get out of dish duty."

"That hardly seems fair, but okay," Presley said, handing over her plate to Allison. The other kids scrambled away from the table.

"I'll help with the dishes," Cody said. "Unless you need me to come outside to help?" he asked Presley with a look that said he really didn't want to play in the snow.

"Nope." Kade stood up and grabbed his plate. "I'm on kid-duty with my fiancée," he said, giving Presley a wink.

It was silly to feel so giddy hearing him call her his fiancée. She hoped her stupid love-sick grin didn't reveal how much she wished their engagement wasn't temporary.

"I hope you two don't have kids right away," Devon said, taking Blake from Jamie. "It's really nice having the fun uncle and aunt team."

Presley saw Kade's eyes widen slightly before he ducked his head to help Lucas clean up the spaghetti sauce from the little boy's face. Each time one of his family members talked about the future, Presley's guilt over their deception increased. She was growing to love this family so much. They would hate her when she broke off the engagement. Her gut twisted at the thought. She was totally making Kade do it. No way was she going to be the one to end things.

"If they wait too long," Jamie said, then their kids will be so much younger than ours."

"True," Stacie said. "It would be nice to have a little cousin close to our baby's age."

Color infused Presley's cheeks as Kade's siblings discussed their future children as if they were a done deal. Kade glanced up, and their eyes met. "Sorry," he mouthed.

What was he sorry about? Ignoring her this morning, or was he sorry because they were lying to his family? "It's fine," she mouthed back. It wasn't really fair to make him the bad guy. Not when he was doing this as a favor for her. When the time came, she would take all the blame for ending their relationship.

Allison chimed in with her own advice on when to have kids. The conversation needed to stop. Kade's mother was so uptight she looked like she was about to snap.

"Would you guys stop talking like we're not here," Kade grumbled. "And stop with the family planning too."

"Kade's right, girls." Marilyn scooted away from the table. "They're not in any rush to get married," she said, dabbing a napkin to the corner of her pinched lips. "So stop pushing them."

An awkward silence settled over the room. Even the kids were quiet as Marilyn took her husband's plate that was still untouched and headed toward his office. Ben had gotten an important phone call before he could eat and hadn't returned.

"Sorry," Jamie said. "We're being way too nosy."

"Yeah, you are," Kade said, throwing a wadded up napkin at Jamie, but it fell short and landed on her plate.

"What did I miss?" Greg said, holding Maddie's hand. He'd taken her to the bathroom a few minutes earlier.

"Nothing," Kade said. "Presley and I are taking the kids out to build a snowman. Want to come?"

"Is that a trick question?" Greg asked.

"No," Kade said, taking Lucas by the hand, "because apparently having kids makes you no fun."

"Huh?" Greg asked with confusion as Kade walked out of the dining room.

"Somebody's cranky," Stacie said. She looked at Presley. "He must need attention from you since you've spent so much time with our kids."

Was Kade feeling neglected? Presley wasn't sure why that made her so happy. "I love your kids."

"I know," Stacie said. "We all love you too."

Warmth filled Presley's chest like she'd swallowed a cup of hot cocoa. They loved her? She glanced at Jamie and Allison, who were both nodding their head in agreement. "That is the sweetest thing anyone has ever said to me," Presley said. Her voice cracked, and she blinked away the burning sensation pressing against the back of her eyelids. If only she could talk to Kade's sisters to see if they had any advice to offer about how she could win their brother's affections.

"Can we go outside now?" Jenny said, tugging on Presley's hand.

"Sure, sweetie." Presley took the little girl by the hand. "Let's go get our snow stuff on."

"That is a job for more than one person," Jamie said, standing up. "Stacie, and I will get the kids ready while you go get your stuff."

Presley was grateful for the chance to be alone so she could think. She headed upstairs to change into her winter clothes, wishing she had someone to talk to. Brynlee was doing wedding stuff with her mom while Travis went golfing with his future father-in-law. Presley knew Brynlee would call her back if she texted her. She would have to keep things to herself for now.

Knocking on the adjoining bathroom door, Presley walked in when nobody answered. The last person she wanted to see was Jillian. Touching up her makeup, Presley braided her hair into two plaits and then put on a navy blue beanie. Grabbing her ski coat, she opened her bedroom door and saw Jillian standing outside as if waiting for her.

"Feeling better?" Presley asked.

"Yes," Jillian said with a smirk. "Kade came to my room and gave me something for my upset stomach. He was so sweet."

Presley refrained from telling Jillian that she knew exactly why Kade had come to her room. "I'm glad he helped you," Presley said, keeping her voice light.

Jillian's brown eyes cooled like iced coffee. That wasn't the reaction she'd hoped to get. "Are you going somewhere?" she asked.

Presley shouldn't provoke Jillian, especially knowing she would tattle on her to Kade's mother. "Kade and I are building a snowman with the kids."

"Oh, good," Jillian said. "Marilyn said she was worried the two of you were fighting since you spend most of your time with the kids instead of Kade."

Ouch. Marilyn had said all that? So maybe her gratitude to Presley about playing with the grandchildren was because she wasn't spending time with Kade?

"We aren't fighting," Presley said. "But thank you for being concerned."

"I'm not concerned," Jillian said, clearly talking about something else entirely. "Kade and I have a connection that goes back a long time. I know everything will work out."

Presley hated knowing that when she and Kade broke up, Jillian would be there waiting in the wings. She was saved from replying when Jenny and Laura raced down the hall to see if she was ready.

"See you later," Presley said as she took each girl by the hand and left Jillian standing there. The girls chatted happily, helping Presley to focus on something else other than Jillian.

Since Allison decided to keep Brooklyn and Maddie inside, Presley only had the twins. Kade and Lucas had already started on their snowman by the time she and girls made it outside. Feeling a little peeved with Kade, Presley led the twins to another section to make their own snowman.

"Hey," Kade called out. "Aren't you going to help us?"

"We're making our own," she answered without looking at him.

"Why?" he asked, sounding annoyed.

Good. She was annoyed with him too. "Because we want to." She got Jenny and Laura started on the head while she focused on the bottom.

She'd managed to get a good base going when she felt something hard and cold hit her on the back. Whirling around, she saw Kade was forming another snowball to throw at her. "You better not throw that at me."

A slow smile curved his mouth. "Or what?" he said as he hurled the snowball, hitting her squarely in the chest.

"You are dead," she growled, scooping up some snow and packing it together. She threw the snowball and only grazed his sleeve because he ducked out of the way.

"I thought the Princess Warrior would have better aim than that," Kade said, throwing another snowball and hitting her in the butt as she bent over to gather up more snow.

Lucas, Jenny, and Laura wanted in on the fun and started making their own snowballs. Presley dodged Kade's next attempt and rushed him, hitting him in the chest. "Gotcha," she said with a laugh. He already had another snowball ready and lobbed it at her. She ducked so it skimmed the top of her hat. "Missed," she said, hitting him in the arm with a snowball Laura handed to her.

"I did that on purpose." He hurled another snowball, but it went wide without hitting any part of her.

"Missed again," she said, sticking her tongue out at him.

Laughing, he had another snowball ready and hit her shoulder, followed by another one that hit her in the arm. Before she could form another snowball, Kade hit her again. Presley made her snowball extra big and then chased after him, hitting him on the back of the neck. The shocked look on his face was motivation to snag one of Jenny's snowballs.

"Let me get the snow out of my collar," he said, dodging her next throw. He moved toward the house and reached behind him, trying to get the snow out.

"I don't think that's a valid snowball fight rule for a timeout." Presley started making another big snowball as she walked toward him.

"There are rules?" he said, abandoning his objective to make another snowball. The snow wasn't as deep by the porch, so he had to bend down again. Presley still hadn't thrown her snowball. She wanted to be close enough to make sure she got him. "Or are they more like guidelines, love?" he asked, sounding like Jack Sparrow.

It reminded her of the hot kisses they'd shared, which only fueled her frustration with this situation. She wanted Kade and not just for pretend. She wanted him to want her too. He straightened up, and she threw the snowball in a straight line. Before it made contact, Kade ducked just as someone stepped out on the porch. In horror, Presley watched as her oversized snowball smacked Marilyn Miles right on the forehead.

CHAPTER 14

KADE

K ade winced when the snowball made contact with his mother's head. She made a grunting sound as her knees buckled, and she crumpled to the ground, landing on her back, so her head rested on the foyer's wood floor.

"Mom, are you okay?" Kade asked, rushing to her side. His mom was holding a hand over her forehead and shaking. Kade was worried she was having a seizure or something.

"I'm so sorry," Presley said, coming to his side. "I didn't mean to hit her." She sounded like she was on the verge of tears.

"It was an accident," he said, leaning in closer to his mom. Was she crying?

"Did I kill her?" Presley asked. "Please tell me I didn't kill her."

His mother made a strangled noise, and that's when he realized she was laughing. *Laughing?* Kade couldn't remember if that was a sign of a head injury or not. "You didn't kill her," he assured Presley.

"What's wrong with Grammy?" Laura asked with Jenny and Lucas right behind her. "Is she dead?"

His mom snorted a laugh and then giggled. Now Kade really was worried about her. He took her by the wrist to count her pulse. Her heart rate was a little rapid, but nothing to be concerned about. "Can you tell me what day it is?" he asked.

"A really, really unfortunate one," Presley answered, which only made his mom laugh harder.

"I was asking my mom," Kade said with a chuckle of his own.

"Mom, what happened?" Allison said, kneeling next to their mother.

Jamie and Stacie appeared next, along with Ben.

"Marilyn!" Ben said, forcing Allie to move so he could kneel next to his wife. Confusion crossed his stepdad's features as he looked at Kade. "Is she laughing?"

Kade shrugged since the question sent his mom into another round of giggling.

"Marilyn?" Ben said. "I'm worried about you, sweetheart."

"I'm fine." Kade's mom hiccupped one last laugh and took Ben's hand to sit up. Her forehead had a red mark in the center that was the size of an egg. Kade didn't see any swelling yet, and it hadn't broken the skin.

"What happened?" Ben asked as his mom wiped at a few tears underneath her bottom lashes.

"I'm not quite sure," his mom said.

"I started a snowball fight, and she accidentally got hit," Kade said. He wanted to claim ownership of the snowball, but Presley beat him to it.

"I'm so sorry, Mrs. Miles," Presley said, worrying her bottom lip. "I was aiming for Kade."

His mom sobered with only a hint of a smile on her face. Kade worried about what was coming next as his mother made direct eye contact with Presley. "I don't remember the last time I was hit with a snowball."

Presley's face paled as white as the snow covering the ground. "I'm very sorry, Mrs. Miles," Presley said again. "Is there anything I can do for you?"

"Yes," his mom answered in a kind voice. "You can call me Marilyn."

"I can?" Presley asked with wide eyes. "I mean, thank you." She swallowed. "Marilyn."

Shocked, Kade observed his mother from a paramedic standpoint rather than as her son, trying to figure out if she really was suffering from a head injury. "Mom, do you know what year it is?" he asked.

His mother narrowed her eyes and gave him the year, month, date, and day of the week. "I'm fine," she said, getting to her feet with the help of his stepdad. "I was more startled than injured."

Kade stood up and noticed Jillian hovering in the background. With her lips pressed into a tight line, she appeared to be in pain. Guilt pressed down on him for his uncharitable thoughts that she was faking her illness. He wished things weren't so strained between them. They had been good friends at one time, but he didn't feel comfortable talking to her. Not when she wanted more from him than he could give.

Jillian's eyes shifted and connected with his. She no longer looked in pain. She looked angry. Maybe he should start a snowball fight with her too. It had worked to get Presley out of her mood. To be fair, he'd been in a mood also. He was frustrated with his family because they had fallen in love with Presley. Sure, they thought she was his fiancée, but it was complicating everything.

And now the last holdout—his mother—appeared to have fallen for Presley's bubbly personality. It was a wonder his mother had resisted Presley so far. She was like radiant sunshine bursting through dark clouds and warming everything around her.

"Marilyn," Jillian said, coming around to his mom's other side. "I have the perfect mask to help with the redness and reduce the swelling."

"I have swelling?" his mom said, touching her forehead with the tips of her fingers.

"No," Kade said. Then he looked at her forehead again. "Maybe a little, but it didn't break the skin."

Jillian threaded her hand through his mom's arm and smiled at Kade. "Leave your mother to me, Mr. Paramedic." She winked at him as if she hadn't just glared daggers at him a few seconds earlier. "I'm feeling much better, by the way," she added. "Thank you again for taking care of me."

Huh? He hadn't done anything other than giving her a couple of Zofran and a Gatorade, telling her to keep hydrated and get plenty of rest. He hadn't touched her or examined her as he was sure his mother had hoped. He only crossed the threshold of Jillian's room to set the medication and drink on the nightstand.

"Come inside, kids," Allison said when Lucas and the twins started complaining about being cold. She and Jamie herded the children into the mudroom to change out of their wet clothes, leaving Stacie with Kade and Presley.

"Did you two kiss and makeup?" Stacie asked with a smirk.

"Did we need to?" Kade asked, not that he wouldn't mind kissing Presley again, but he wasn't ready for the harassment to start again. He needed to think about what to do with his growing feelings for her. He wasn't sure if it was the real deal or just circumstances and some super-hot chemistry.

"We weren't fighting," Presley said. "Unless you count a snowball fight." She turned to look at Kade. "Which I totally won."

"Right," Kade said with a laugh. "Except for that last snowball hit my mom instead of me."

"You're hilarious," Presley said, sticking her tongue out at him again. "I'm going to take a hot shower and change my clothes."

Once Presley left, Kade could tell his sister had something else on her mind. "What?" he asked, unzipping his coat. He was sweating now that he was inside, and his adrenaline spike was over. "I can tell you want to say something."

"I just don't understand you and Presley is all," Stacie said, eyeing him with speculation. "You are the strangest engaged couple I've ever been around."

Kade drew in a sharp breath and stared at Stacie. Did she know he and Presley weren't really engaged? "Why do you say that?" he asked.

He had to admit that if Stacie did know this was all a sham, it would make him feel better. He needed someone other than Presley to talk to. Travis was usually his go-to, but since this was all about his little sister and that Kade might possibly be falling in love with her, that wasn't an option.

"I don't know." Stacie pursed her bottom lip in thought. "You two have this underlying sexual tension, but then you hardly ever touch each other."

"We're engaged not married," Kade said, pulling at the collar of his shirt. It felt like it was suddenly trying to choke him.

"I'm not talking about doing you know what," Stacie said. "Greg and I couldn't keep our hands off each other when we were engaged. We always were holding hands and stealing kisses." She looked at Kade through narrowed eyes. "Honestly, when you and Presley kissed under the mistletoe, it almost seemed like it was the first time."

Dang. His sister was good. Kade desperately wanted to confide in Stacie, but with her pregnancy hormones all over the place, he wasn't sure he could trust her.

"It's kind of awkward with an ex-girlfriend breathing down my neck, and Mom pushing Jillian and me to get married so she and Mrs. Hastings can share grandchildren."

"True." Stacie wound a finger through her blonde hair. "But I think Presley might have won Mom over."

So he wasn't imagining things. His mom was warming up to Presley. "You think?" he asked, not sure why his stomach felt like he'd swallowed a hornet's nest, and they had been let loose.

"Are you nervous about proposing on television?" Stacie asked.

"A little." Kade swallowed hard. "It kind of makes it all real, you know?"

"Real?" she asked. "Are you having second thoughts?"

Yes. No. He was so confused. "I'm brave enough to admit that falling in love with Presley scares me to death."

There. He'd said it out loud. In a roundabout way, he admitted he was scared and that he was falling for Presley.

"Kade, I know you've always been wary of marriage because of your birth father. But you've seen how happy Mom and Dad are." She playfully slugged him in the arm. "And all three of your sisters are happily married to some great guys. Greg was a confirmed bachelor when he met me, but it only took a couple of dates to change his mind, and we're happy." She grinned. "He makes me crazy sometimes, but I love being married to him."

"I know." He looked away and ran a hand through his damp hair. "Presley is amazing, isn't she?"

"Yes," Stacie said, smiling at him when he looked back at her, "she is amazing. And beautiful and kind and has a killer body. You would be really stupid if you let her get away because you're getting cold feet."

Kade considered his sister for a long moment. Did she know, or was she just sensing his angst? "What if it doesn't work out?"

"What if it does?" Stacie countered back.

"Honey?" Greg said, holding up a familiar looking package. "Don't go ballistic, but Maddie found your chocolate covered cinnamon bears."

"She ate them all?" Stacie asked incredulously.

"No, she freely shared them with her cousins."

"Ah man," Stacie said, taking the empty package from Greg. "Where are we going to get more cinnamon bears?"

"I've got a mostly full bag in the car," Kade said with a laugh.

"Thanks, man," Greg said, giving Kade a fist bump.

"Bless you," Stacie said. "You just saved our marriage."

"What are you talking about, woman?" Greg said, bumping his wife in the shoulder. "We're solid."

"Yeah," she said, kissing him on the mouth, "we are."

Envy for what Stacie and Greg had wormed its way into Kade's already screwed up thinking. He knew Stacie and Greg loved each other, but they'd had some pretty verbal arguments over the years. Still, even though they'd married young, they always made up and were seemingly happy. He wanted to ask Greg if he'd ever felt trapped or like he'd made a mistake but it probably wasn't the best timing to ask him something like that what with his wife pregnant and holding an empty bag of chocolate.

"Oh, I almost forgot," Greg said. "Since the movie was sold out, and Jillian is feeling better, Mom decided the talent show is back on."

"Yeah, that's what she was coming out to tell you all when the snowball incident happened," Stacie said. "I still can't believe Mom was laughing about that. Guess that shows you how special your lady is," she added with a wink.

Presley was special. Kade hadn't ever met anyone quite like her before. No one had ever made him seriously consider marriage. Was he ready to take a chance and make their relationship real? It's not like they had to get engaged. Okay, he knew they were getting engaged but it was for the show. It didn't mean they had to get married right away.

Some of the tension eased out of Kade's shoulders. The talent show would give him a little time to mull things over. Plus, he'd finally get to see what Presley was doing for her talent. Now if he could only get out of playing the guitar for Jillian. Maybe he'd get lucky, and she'd be too mad at him to want him to accompany her. Even better, maybe she'd take the next flight out and go to Belgium and have Christmas with her parents.

CHAPTER 15

PRESLEY

Something was bothering Kade. While he wasn't as moody and grumpy as this afternoon, he was definitely distracted. He'd hardly looked at Presley since she'd joined the family in the great room for the talent show. She wondered if he was coming down with the same thing Blake had. The little boy had a low-grade fever, along with a stomach bug. Or maybe it was the fact that Kade's mother didn't hate her anymore. They weren't best friends or anything, but she was much kinder to her. Even so, it meant one more person that would be hurt when she and Kade broke things off. Presley, being the primary victim.

If only Brynlee would text her back. Presley didn't want to bother her and Travis, but she'd sent out an SOS text for help. Brynlee was the romance reader and might have a suggestion about what to do. Presley had no idea if she was the one who needed to say something or if she should wait for Kade to say something. But what if he didn't feel the same way? What if he wasn't interested in really dating her?

Sighing, she let her eyes drift over to Kade. He was sitting by the fireplace and strumming his guitar. She let her gaze linger on him, appreciating how handsome he looked with the shadow of dark whiskers covering his jaw. He'd have to shave when he went back to work, but she liked the rugged look on him. The wool sweater he had on made him look like a model for the cover of an outdoor magazine.

Before she looked away, Kade lifted his face and caught her staring at him. Their eyes connected and, even from this distance, the pull of attraction reached out and twined them together in a way she'd never experienced before.

Presley fingered her mother's wedding ring as she finally acknowledged the truth. She'd done what she told herself not to do and was completely and wholeheartedly in love with Kade Hunter. She wanted to be his wife and have his babies. She wanted to compete in gingerbread house contests with him and then give him the winning prize because she adored him so much. She wanted to sing a duet with him, even though she had zero vocal talent. She wanted him, and it hurt that he didn't feel the same way.

One more day and the camera crew was coming to film their proposal. But Presley didn't know if she could go through with it. The innocent falsehood was morphing into something so much bigger because she'd also fallen in love with Kade's family.

Dropping her gaze, she picked up Maddie, who was tugging on her shirt. "Hey, baby girl," Presley said, scooping the little girl in her arms. Stacie had just bathed her, and the child smelled so good. Burying her face in the soft curls, she inhaled the sweet baby smell. Kade had asked her if she wanted kids, and, like an idiot, she'd immediately jumped to the conclusion that he was asking if she wanted to have kids with him. It was so embarrassing, but he'd let her off the hook and then surprised her by admitting he wanted kids too. Why was he telling her he wanted kids? She wanted to believe it was because he saw a real future with her, but he sure had a funny way of showing it if he did.

"Grammy," Laura asked Marilyn. "When can Jenny and me do our dance?"

Marilyn glanced at the stairs with concern. She may be warming to Presley but it didn't mean that she loved Jillian any less. "In a minute, sweetie," Marilyn said. "Jillian will be here soon." At least the red mark on her forehead was gone. Whatever stuff Jillian had done must work miracles. Marilyn's skin looked flawless and beautiful.

Lucas raced across the floor, zooming the paper airplane Kade had made for him earlier. The kids were all getting restless, waiting for the talent show to start. Or rather for Jillian to make an appearance.

Movement caught her eye, and Presley glanced up at the stairs to see Jillian coming down. She looked beautiful, her dark hair contrasting with the off-white, mock turtleneck sweater paired with leather pants that hugged every perfect curve of her body.

Jillian's cool eyes rested on Presley, her red lips parting in a smile that looked kind of like the Grinch when he got an awful idea. Animosity glittered in Jillian's eyes before she averted her attention to where Kade sat.

Presley had tried to be a friend even though Jillian wasn't making the same effort. Her attitude was making it really hard for Presley to feel sorry for her. Her comment a couple of hours earlier still stung when Jillian told her she really needed to try a little harder to look nice. Presley was wearing what she usually wore. Yoga pants with an oversized sweatshirt. She had just gotten out of the shower and hadn't done her hair or makeup when Jillian informed her she needed a stylist to improve her image.

Presley's image was something Zuri was always after her to change. This morning, she'd checked in with her and had a hissy fit with Presley's wardrobe choice for the romantic proposal. Apparently, the soft gray cashmere sweater and black jeans Presley planned on wearing wasn't camera worthy. Zuri was prepared to fly in with wardrobe choices of her own until Presley sent her a picture of the sexy red dress Brynlee had packed for her.

"You're soft," Maddie said, running her little hands over Presley's sweater. Since she wasn't wearing the cashmere sweater for the kick-off special, she decided to wear it for the talent show. She was glad she'd dressed up a little, and not because of Jillian. Presley was doing it for herself. And maybe Kade might take notice too.

"Jillian, I'm so glad you're feeling better," Marilyn said, wrapping her in a motherly embrace.

Presley had a perfect view of Jillian's face. She gave Presley a haughty smile as if to say she'd won. The urge to stick out her tongue was too much, so Presley buried her face back in Maddie's curls and spun the little girl around, making her giggle. Soon, she had Brooklyn at her side, begging for her to spin her around. Presley loved these little girls. She loved all of Kade's nieces and nephews.

Hopefully, Brynlee and Travis wouldn't wait too long to have kids. Thinking about it reminded her of Kade's sisters and their advice on when they should have children. Presley wished with all her heart that her children could grow up with cousins close to their age. She and Travis didn't have any cousins, since both her parents were only children. After spending time with Kade's large family, she knew she wanted to have at least three kids.

"Welcome to the annual Mile's Family Talent Show," Ben said. He went on to say how grateful he and Marilyn were to have such a wonderful family and that the talent show wasn't a competition but a way to share in one another's talents.

Jillian cut Presley a look that said this was all about a competition, and she intended to come out the winner. She was sitting next to Marilyn and made a show of whispering something to Kade's mother that had Marilyn leaning in to give Jillian an affectionate one-armed hug.

Ignoring her, Presley snuggled up to Maddie and Brooklyn as the opening act started with Greg, Devon, and Cody in a lip-sync battle against their wives to Christmas songs. The girls won since most of the time the guys forgot the right lyrics. But the men's dance moves made up for the poorly executed singing, making everyone laugh.

Next, Jenny and Laura performed a hip-hop dance that was so cute it should be illegal. Maddie and Brooklyn danced next. It was simple, and they forgot most of the steps but also very cute. Lucas was next with a magic show that wasn't half bad for a six-year-old.

"Next," Ben said, looking down at his program. "We have a special musical number from Jillian and Kade."

Presley's stomach lurched when she heard the name combination of Kade and Jillian like they were Britain's William and Kate. Just yesterday, Kade had told her that he wasn't singing with Jillian, but he'd obviously changed his mind. Unable to look at him, she was grateful that Brooklyn was now sitting on her lap.

Presley did her best to keep her emotions in check, but it felt like a large stone was lodged at the base of her throat as Kade took his guitar and sat on a stool next to Jillian. It was stupid to feel like Kade betrayed her, but that's exactly what it felt like.

Jillian introduced the song "Where are you Christmas" by Faith Hill. It was one of Presley's favorite songs. She had a feeling she'd never be able to listen to it again with the same feelings. Jillian the Grinch had stolen something else from her.

Even though she didn't want to look, she couldn't help lifting her head when Kade started picking the melody out on the guitar. Jillian was standing so close to him they were almost touching.

Jillian's voice was even better out of the shower. It was perfect and clear, completely captivating the audience. Even the grandkids were mesmerized. Kade looked up frequently, and each time, Presley made sure she wasn't staring at him. He never sang, which made her feel a little better. Singing a duet was so much more intimate.

When the song ended, Presley clapped along with the rest of the family. Kade started to stand up but Jillian placed her hand on his knee. "I know many of you remember the duet Kade and I sang a couple of years ago. We'd like to sing that for you now."

Kade's mouth pressed into a thin line, and he shook his head. Jillian was prepared. She tapped on the screen of her tablet and connected a video call to her parents. "Please," she said, holding up the screen. "Mom and Dad are feeling lonely and requested we sing our song."

Our song? The stone pressing against Presley's throat dropped to her stomach with a thud. She wasn't sure she could sit here much longer without crying.

Kade's mother was delighted to see her best friend. She jumped up and took the tablet from Jillian. "We miss you both so much," she said with tears in her eyes. Then she looked at Kade. "Please sing it with her, sweetheart. It would mean so much to Olivia and Peter."

The muscle in Kade's jaw tightened as he made eye contact with Presley. He seemed to be seeking her permission. She wasn't sure why and couldn't tell him no. Giving a slight nod of her head, she saw the lines in his face soften as he sat back down on the stool and picked up his guitar.

The song was torturous and wonderful at the same time, which really messed with Presley's emotions. Kade and Jillian sang in perfect harmony and looked good together. She hated feeling so jealous but couldn't help it. Her talent seemed so stupid now after listening to Jillian's incredible voice blend with Kade's.

Presley thought about faking a stomachache and going to her room. She wasn't quick enough to execute her plan. Ben stood up and announced her as the final talent, inviting all of the children to come sit on the floor together as Presley had requested.

It wouldn't have been so bad, but Jillian's parents didn't hang up. They wanted to see Kade's fiancée since they'd heard so much about her. Presley could only guess what they'd heard from Jillian.

Ignoring the stern looking faces on the iPad, Presley started telling the kids a story about a lost balloon that didn't know who it was or where it belonged. She hadn't made balloon animals for a long time, but the simple ones were easy, which she stuck to. As predicted, the kids loved calling out what animal they wanted. Lucas wanted a dinosaur but settled for a giraffe since a dinosaur required more balloons than she had. As she twisted and tweaked the yellow balloon, she continued with her story, making it up as she went along.

Handing off the balloon creation to Lucas, Presley caught a glimpse of Kade sitting on the chair behind Jenny and Laura. Leaning forward with his hands clasped between his legs, he stared steadily at her, his blue eyes unreadable and a small smile playing at his lips.

Flustered, Presley avoided eye contact with him and continued with her story. Still, she could feel his gaze on her, and it made her feel as jittery as the kids after eating the bag of chocolate covered cinnamon bears. The twins wanted dogs, and Presley suggested a butterfly for Maddie. Brooklyn wanted a giraffe like her brother but was happy when Presley made her a monkey. Blake was asleep, which was good since Presley had run out of balloons.

Presley was bombarded with applause and whistles from the audience when she finished the story. Although she told herself not to look at Kade, her eyes drifted over the heads of the children and connected with his baby blues. Awareness crackled like the logs in the fireplace, heating her to the core.

"Kids," Allison called out. "Let's get a picture of you and your balloon animals with Presley."

Presley blinked, and the connection broke as Kade's nieces and nephews huddled in close around her. Presley's lips quivered as she smiled for the camera. She loved these little people so much. She loved this family so much. Her eyes shifted slightly, meeting Kade's gaze again. And she loved Kade so much it made her heart physically hurt.

"Can I hire you for the twin's birthday?" Jamie asked when the photo op ended. "It's in a couple of weeks and always so hard to do right after Christmas."

"Yeah, and maybe give us a family discount too," Devon added.

"I'd love to do it," Presley said, wondering if she and Kade would still be together by then. They hadn't really discussed when the breakup was going to happen. "And I won't charge you anything."

Allison and Stacie both hugged her and asked if she'd consider to birthday parties for their kids when it came time. Lucas and Brooklyn were summer babies, and Maddie's birthday was in April. Presley didn't have the heart to tell them no, even though she knew that she and Kade would have broken up long before that time.

Kade came up behind her and slipped his arm around Presley's waist. He hadn't touched her like this today, and the physical contact was almost too much. Every point of contact sent sparks of electricity through her body. She leaned into him in case her knees gave out and caught the tangy scent of his cologne. Why did he have to smell so good?

"Mind if I steal my fiancée for a minute?" Kade asked his sisters.

"Are you taking her on another tour of the house?" Stacie asked, using air quotes.

"As a matter of fact I am," Kade said. "I forgot to show her the hot tub and sauna."

"Ooh, hot tubbing without kids," Jamie teased, wiggling her eyebrows up and down. "I remember those days fondly. We'll keep everyone else away so you two can have some alone time together."

"I didn't bring a swimsuit," Presley said, wondering what Kade was up to. He'd already showed her the hot tub and sauna. She'd regretted not listening to Brynlee to pack her bikini because she would've loved to sneak out of her room last night for a soak in the heated water.

"Check the room next to the sauna," Allie said. "Mom keeps a lot of swimsuits there, and I'm sure one will fit you."

"Good idea." Kade took Presley by the hand and led her out of the family room. They passed Jillian and Marilyn who were still video chatting with Mr. and Mrs. Hastings. Knowing the kind of look Jillian would give her, Presley purposely didn't look at the two women and was relieved when she and Kade made it out without Jillian inserting herself between them.

"You already showed me the hot tub," Presley said, once they were away from his family.

"I know." He opened the door to an office that doubled as a library. "But I needed a good excuse to get you alone." Pulling her inside, he closed the door and locked it behind him.

"So you can do what?" she asked suspiciously when he didn't turn the lights on. Maybe he was going to tell her that he and Jillian were getting back together, and he wanted it dark so he didn't have to see her reaction.

"This." Kade took her face in his palms and caught her mouth in a kiss that melted every bone in her body. As his lips moved over hers, Presley figured this wasn't a prelude to a breakup or an announcement he and Jillian were an item again. She probably should end the kiss and find out what was going on in that handsome head of his, but she wasn't thinking so clearly anymore.

Need and desire made her want to be closer. Wrapping her arms around his waist, she melted against him, returning his kiss with a recklessness she didn't know she had inside her. It was a desperate kiss as if she knew that this might be her only chance to really kiss the man she loved. With a growl, Kade slid his hands into her hair, curving it around her neck and demanded more from her mouth, kissing her with a hunger that drugged her.

The door rattled behind them, followed by a swift knock. Kade groaned again as he ended the kiss and pressed his forehead to Presley's. "Whoever is at the door better have a good excuse," he said, his breathing as ragged as hers.

"Ben," Marilyn called out. "The door's locked. Can you please come open it for me?"

Presley's warm body flushed cold with foreboding. She was about to be caught in the dark with Kade. His mom may have forgiven her for throwing a snowball at her, but what would she think about a girl who willingly locked herself in the library for a make-out session during a family Christmas party?

"We need to hide," Presley whispered, hearing the panic in her voice.

"Not sure we'll both fit under the desk," Kade said with a chuckle. "Because there isn't anywhere else to hide but there."

"Then let me hide, and you cover for me." She gasped when she heard the doorknob rattle again. "They'll know what we've been doing," Presley hissed.

"We're engaged, so it's kind of expected that we like to kiss," Kade said.

"Ha, you've practically ignored me all day." Presley squeezed her eyes shut, even though it was too dark for Kade to see. She hadn't meant to say that out loud.

"I know, and I'm sorry," he said in a husky voice. "I—"

Whatever Kade was about to say was cut off when the door opened and light flooded the room.

CHAPTER 16

K ade blinked at the bright light, wishing his mom could've given him at least five more minutes alone with Presley so he could talk to her. He looked at Presley's swollen lips, instantly craving another taste. Okay, so maybe thirty more minutes since he wasn't done kissing her yet. But then they really needed to talk.

"Oh my," his mother said, coving her heart with her hand. "I didn't know anyone was in here."

Presley made a noise of distress as she stepped away from him, not getting too far since Kade kept a hold of her hand. There was no use pretending they hadn't been caught making out, but he had to try. "It's okay," Kade said. "We came in here to call Presley's brother and must have locked the door."

His mom stared at him steadily, and he knew she wasn't buying it. Kade just hoped she didn't revert back to giving Presley the cold shoulder after Jillian tricked him into singing with her while her parents watched. "I'm sorry to interrupt the phone call," she said, giving them a tight smile.

"We didn't actually call yet so it's fine," Kade said, sticking to the truth. Really, he and Presley were adults and didn't need his mother's permission to find a few moments of privacy together.

"The kids want a bedtime story," his mom said, crossing the floor to pick up a children's Christmas book from the desk. "And then Stacie and Greg have a new game for the adults."

"I like adult games," Kade said with a straight face. He felt Presley gasp, and she squeezed his hand tightly. "I brought a new card game we should try too."

"You're not too old to be on Santa's naughty list, young man," his mom said, her lips twitching at the corners. "Make sure you bring that new game in case we want to give it a try."

"Yes, ma'am."

Clutching the book to her chest, his mother's focus shifted to Presley. "Thank you for sharing such a fun talent with our family, Presley. The children loved it."

"Thank you," Presley said, her voice soft and filled with emotion. "I had fun too."

His mom looked at Kade again. "Don't be too long," she said on the way back out of the library. Then she did something that completely floored Kade. His mom turned the light off and pulled the door closed.

"Wow, she must really like you," Kade said, still stunned by his mother's actions. Was this the final sign that he needed to broach the topic he'd brooded over all day long? He had to believe it was. He found Presley's hand in the dark and reeled her to him. "I like you too."

He wasn't quite ready to say the other "L" word and mean it in the way he should. Besides, he felt like it was only right that he and Presley date for a little while. But this time for real. And, if things continued on the path they were on right now, then he wanted to give her Grandma Hunter's ring along with his heart. Did the idea of getting married still scare him? Absolutely, but it scared him even more to think of Presley eventually finding someone else.

"I like you too," she said with a heaviness he couldn't decipher without seeing her face. "But we can't keep doing this."

"Sneaking off to make out?" he teased.

"No." She swatted him on the chest and then left her palm to rest there. "Kade, your family is amazing, and they think we're really getting married. I didn't count on our arrangement hurting anyone else."

He felt the same way. His sisters would kill him if he didn't give this relationship a shot. At one time or another, all three of them had warned him not to mess this up. "I know, I didn't either."

"I'm not sure I can go through with it."

For a moment, Kade felt like he couldn't catch his breath. Was she saying she didn't want to be with him? Or was she talking about the fake proposal tomorrow?

"Hang on." He let go of her and made his away across the floor to the light switch. He needed to see her face before they discussed this any further. "That's better," he said as the room brightened.

"Is it?" Presley glowered at him, blinking a few times as her eyes adjusted to the light.

He smiled and took her hand, leading her over to the leather recliner and pulled her onto his lap. "We need to talk."

"Yes, I suppose we do." She bit her bottom lip, something he noticed she did whenever she was distressed.

Slanting forward, he placed a light kiss to her mouth until she released her lower lip and kissed him back. He allowed himself to linger for a moment more before moving his mouth to kiss her forehead. "You're amazing," he said, edging back to look into her eyes.

"Thanks." Presley had one hand around his neck, absently fingering his hair brushing against the collar of his sweater. "I think you are too."

"I'm sorry I've been so distant today," Kade said, not sure how wise it was to have this conversation in such close proximity. Her touch was driving him wild, and he wanted to kiss her again. "I've had a lot on my mind."

Presley's fingers stilled, resting at the base of his neck. "Is it the proposal tomorrow?" she asked.

"Yes and no." He swallowed, gathering up the courage to tell her that he was done pretending.

"You don't have to go through with it, Kade," she said, her chin dropping down so he couldn't see her eyes.

"I'm not backing out of the deal." He waited until she was looking at him again before he continued. "I know your brother might not like it, but I want to date you for real." He held his breath, hoping she felt the same way.

Presley's eyes widened. "For real?" She nervously moistened her lips with the tip of her tongue. "You really do?"

"Yeah." Now it was his turn to feel nervous. "If that's what you want too."

Her blue eyes held his for what seemed like an eternity. Then her mouth curved up into the sweetest smile. "Yes," she said with a light laugh. She leaned in and kissed him on the mouth, which didn't last long enough. "Do you know how much easier it will be when the camera crew is here to film our proposal now that I know it's real?"

Wait a sec...proposal real? Kade's throat constricted as if somebody had slipped a rope around his neck and tightened it. He didn't mean the engagement was real just that his feelings for her were genuine. They needed to date and get to know each other as boyfriend and girlfriend before they changed their status to something more permanent. Because what if Presley changed her mind about him? What if he wasn't ready to make that kind of life-long commitment?

Presley's smile fell as she studied his face. "What did I say?" she said, sliding off his lap to stand up. Kade was still processing the conversation in his mind to keep her close to him. "Are you about to break my heart?" she choked out.

Kade glanced at her and felt horrible. Her eyes looked listless and hollow as if someone had snatched the sunshine out of her. "Presley...I—" His gut twisted into a thousand knots as her blue eyes shimmered with tears. The last thing he wanted to do was make her cry.

"You didn't mean it," she said with a sniff. A single tear spilled over her bottom lashes and slid down her smooth cheek.

"I did mean it," he said, standing up beside her. He reached for her hands, but she snatched them back and moved away from him. "This is not going how I planned," Kade said, shoving his hand through his hair. Okay, so he hadn't planned anything out, but he thought he was a better communicator than this. "I meant what I said about us dating for real. I'm just not ready to be engaged." He blew out a harsh breath. "I don't think you're ready for that either."

Hurt flashed in her eyes, and she bit down on her lower lip. A few more tears escaped, trailing down her cheeks. It made him wish Travis was here to punch him in the face. Kade deserved it.

"I don't understand," she said in a shaky voice. "What about the film crew?"

"We'll still go through with the proposal for the show."

"And after?" she questioned softly.

"And after we'll keep dating and see where this goes." He took a step toward, relieved when she didn't back away. Tentatively, he reached out and took her hand. Her fingers were cool to the touch and remained limp. "I care about you. A lot," he said, running his thumb across her knuckles. "I think we have something special but I don't want to rush into anything."

Seconds ticked by, his heart pounding against his sternum as he waited for her response. "I care about you too." Finally, she curled her fingers around his hand. "I don't want to rush you either."

His chest expanded, allowing him to draw in a full breath. "So, we're good?" he asked, giving her hand a gentle squeeze.

"Yes." She gave him a watery smile. "We're good."

"Good." Kade tugged on her hand, and she came to him willingly. "Thank you for giving me a chance."

"Kade, I..." Her gaze flickered away, and she rubbed her lips together. "I'm glad we're giving us a chance too."

He might not be as great of a communicator as he'd thought, but he did know that wasn't what she was going to say. Before he could question her, she looked at him and smiled. "So are going to tell Travis, or do you want me to?"

The invisible noose tightened around his throat again, but he schooled his reaction so it didn't show on his face. Telling Travis was a big deal and one step closer to either making their friendship stronger or breaking it altogether. "I'll tell him." He pulled her in for a hug. "Or maybe we can do it together in case he wants to punch me in the face."

She laughed and slid her arms around his neck. "Chicken." Then she pressed her mouth to his, cutting off his denial about being a chicken.

He let her take the lead, reveling in the softness of her mouth. His hands went to her hips as she slipped her fingers through the hair at his nape, her touch firing along his skin that started a slow burn in his belly. Kade deepened the kiss as his hands slid around to rest at her lower back. Need rushed through him like a torrent of water breaking through a barrier as he pressed his hand against her back to bring her closer. How had he lived without her? Without this?

The image of her sitting in front of his nieces and nephews, captivating them with her story while twisting the balloons into animals, materialized in his mind. She was amazing, and Kade had been captivated too.

Something shifted inside Kade, and that's when he knew. He wanted more. He wanted her forever.

CHAPTER 17

PRESLEY

S tacie let out a low whistle as Presley stepped out of her side of the bathroom and smoothed her palms down the front of the silky red dress. "Do I look okay?"

"Um, you look freaking amazing." Stacie rubbed her baby bump. "I may ask to borrow that dress one day, but don't hold your breath. Not sure if my pre-pregnancy body would've fit in that dress either."

"You're beautiful," Presley said. "I hope I look as good as you do someday if I ever have kids."

"Thanks, but I definitely see little Hunter babies in your future." Stacie wiggled her eyebrows up and down. "When Kade sees you in that dress, he's going to beg you to marry him right then so he can start working on making those babies sooner than later."

"Stacie," Presley said, feeling her cheeks go red. "We're not even engaged." Realizing what she'd said, she quickly added,

"Remember, he's going to propose in..." she glanced at the digital clock on the nightstand. "Thirty minutes."

Stacie studied Presley closely. "Will you tell me the truth if I ask you something?"

Shoot. Did Stacie know something? Presley couldn't lie to her if she came right out and asked if she and Kade were really engaged.

"Yes," Presley answered, her voice quavering with nerves. Part of her wanted Stacie to ask her so she could finally talk to someone. Brynlee still hadn't returned her text or called her. Zuri hadn't either, which made Presley think something was wrong with her phone. She'd lost it last night only to find it wedged between the cushions of the loveseat and turned off. Presley hadn't sent another text to her future sister-in-law. Travis and Brynlee didn't need her drama or intruding on their first Christmas together.

"Did my brother's first proposal totally suck?" Stacie asked.

Presley laughed. Yes, the proposal sucked but it wasn't his fault. "Let's just say that this one will be much more romantic." In her heart, she had high hopes that someday Kade would propose to her one last time. While she wouldn't mind something fun like a flash mob or faking a fire drill, she just wanted it to come from his heart because he loved her. Not liked her or cared about her but really loved her.

Because she loved him. So much. She'd almost told him that she loved him last night but stopped herself in time. He didn't want to rush into anything, and she wasn't going to push him.

"Knock, knock," Jamie said, opening the door a crack. "Can we come in?"

"As long as the *we* isn't Kade," Stacie said.

"Nope, he's downstairs looking like a nervous wreck," Allison said, coming in behind Jamie.

Both women stopped, and their mouths dropped open. "You are going to knock his socks off," Jamie said. "I think the camera guy needs to capture that on film."

"He does," Allison agreed. "I wonder if they'll listen to a civilian's opinion?"

"So the crew is all here?" Presley asked, feeling like she might toss her cookies after all. She spied the garbage can and made her way over to it. "I think I might be sick."

"Don't you dare," Stacie said. "Just take a deep breath and let it out slowly."

"Yeah, you've got this," Allison said. "You're the Princess Warrior, remember?"

She was the Princess Warrior, and her Prince Charming was downstairs waiting to fake propose to her. So maybe this proposal was going to suck just as much as the first non-existent one.

Another knock sounded at the door. "Come in," Presley said, wondering if it was Marilyn. Kade's mom had been a little on the grouchy side today and didn't want the grandkids running around in other areas of the house other than the great room and kitchen. She wanted the house to look perfect, adding more pressure to an already stressful day.

"Come in," Presley said when the knock sounded again. She hoped it wasn't Jillian. Something was up with her. Kade's ex had done a complete one-eighty, acting all nice and sweet to

Presley as if they were BFF's. It had started last night after Presley and Kade came out of the library to play Stacie's new game with everyone. To be honest, it was kind of creepy how nice Jillian was being to Presley. Kade hoped her change of heart was because she finally accepted that he was with Presley now. It was highly unlikely. More like she was plotting her revenge, and being Presley's friend was the best way to do it.

"Hello," a redheaded woman said as she pushed the door and zeroed in on Presley. "I'm Natasha, the director of this segment." She reached out and smoothed a lock of Presley's blonde hair. "I've got a makeup artist out in the hall. She needs to fix a few things, and then we'll be ready to start filming."

"Okay," Presley said as a petite Asian woman came into the room, pulling a large rolling suitcase with her.

"I'm Lilly," she said, setting her suitcase down on the floor. "And you're gorgeous."

"Thank you." Presley watched as Natasha escorted Allison, Jamie, and Stacie out. Allison paused long enough to offer her opinion about capturing Kade's reaction like Presley was wearing a wedding dress, and the videographer wanted to capture the groom's first look.

Natasha grunted something Presley couldn't hear and closed the door. Consulting her iPad, she talked about what was going to happen while Lilly pulled out a white plastic cape and draped it around Presley's neck.

For the next ten minutes, Natasha told her the order they were shooting in. She wanted Kade and Presley alone for the proposal. After that, she wanted to get some footage of them with the family and then ask Kade and Presley a few questions like when they met. Since Presley had already filled out a questionnaire Zuri had forwarded, Natasha handed her a printed script with the answers she and Kade had given. "Mr. Hunter has his copy, so hopefully it will go smoothly." Natasha tapped on her iPad. "We've got families too, so we want to be done before four so my team can be home for Christmas Eve."

"Of course," Presley said, feeling bad they had to be here in the first place. She wasn't sure why they couldn't have done it on another night and just said it was Christmas Eve. At least they were getting an early start. It was only nine-thirty in the morning.

"Lilly, have her ready in ten," Natasha ordered. "Text me when you're ready to come downstairs."

"You got it, Nat," Lilly said, giving Presley a wink. "She's intense but good at what she does," she added after Natasha left them alone in the room.

Eight minutes later, Lilly declared Presley as perfect. After removing the white cape, she loaded her stuff back into the suitcase and then texted Natasha Presley was ready for the camera.

Since Presley had previous experience with being filmed, she kind of knew what to expect. Basically, you did what the director told you to do. Apparently, Natasha had taken Allison's advice. They were staging Kade, so he stood in front of the living room fireplace, waiting for Presley to come up behind him. It was going down exactly like a groom's first look. Presley hoped for a little Christmas magic to grant her wish that someday she would come up behind Kade, wearing a white wedding dress instead of a red cocktail dress.

Standing at the top of the stairs to wait for her cue, Presley automatically went to twist her mother's wedding ring. It felt weird having her finger bare even though she'd only worn the ring for a few days. Glancing down, she rubbed her thumb over the empty space. Would she ever wear another ring there? One that Kade gave her and not the one she'd found tucked away in her mother's jewelry box?

"Places everyone," Natasha called out. "And roll camera."

There were two cameramen working. One a close-up and the other distance. Presley smiled, trying to act natural as she descended the stairs. From the corner of her eyes, she saw part of Kade's family hovering in the other room. Marilyn stood in the front, next to her daughters and Jillian.

"Cut," Natasha called out. "Let's take it from the top, Presley, but this time don't look like your constipated."

Constipated? She'd probably inadvertently made a face when she spied Jillian watching her like a hawk tracks its prey. "Sorry," Presley said before turning to go back up and start over. "I'm just nervous."

"You've got this," Lilly said when Presley reached the top of the stairs.

Presley started down the stairs again, this time focusing on Kade in the other room. She couldn't wait to see him again. After their intense conversation last night, mingled with some pretty hot kissing, she'd expected him to be distant this morning. It was just the opposite. He woke her up early this morning so they could work out in the gym together. After, they'd soaked in the hot tub and talked about some of their best childhood Christmas memories. There had been more kissing involved, but that was cut short when Kade's stepdad joined them after his morning run.

"And cut," Natasha said. "It was perfect."

While the camera, sound, and lighting crews moved into the living room, Lilly came over with a brush and powder and quickly did her magic to make sure Presley's face looked as flawless as Marilyn's.

The director called for the marker and then called out action. Presley's breath caught when she saw Kade standing with his back to her, staring at the flickering fire. His broad shoulders filled out the suit coat to perfection. The assistant director motioned for Kade to slowly turn around. Either Kade was a natural when it came to acting in front of the camera, or he was truly love-struck. It was the only way Presley could describe the look in his eyes as he made a slow perusal over her from the top of her head down to the strappy gold stilettos encasing her feet.

It allowed Presley time to take him in all his glory, leaving her a little love-struck too. He hadn't shaved, something Presley had requested, making him look a little on the dangerous side. Beneath the slim-fitted suit, he wore a crisp white dress shirt and a long, skinny black tie.

"You look so beautiful, Presley," he said in a low sexy voice that shot a jolt of warm energy through her.

"You do too." Wait...she wasn't supposed to say that, but nobody yelled for them to start over, so she took Kade's outstretched hand. "I missed you," she said, totally off-script.

One corner of his mouth edged up into a lopsided grin. "It's only been an hour since we saw each other."

"It feels like forever."

His blue eyes smoldered as they roamed over her face and

settled on her mouth. "It does." Then Kade wrapped an arm around her waist and pulled her to him, lowering his head to give her a long, sensual kiss that had her heart pounding so rapidly she was sure the boom mic overhead would pick it up.

"Cut," Natasha called out.

Kade disregarded the command and let his lips linger for several more seconds. One of the camera guys gave a low whistle when Presley and Kade drew back and stared into each other's eyes.

"That was perfect," Natasha said with a chuckle. "Can somebody bring me a bottle of cold water. It's getting hot in here."

One of her assistants brought her the water, and then they prepped for the proposal. Instead of a candlelit dinner, Presley and Kade decided to slow dance to Michael Bublè singing "White Christmas."

Kade took Presley in his arms as the music cued and pulled her close, his warm body sending an enticing tingle across her skin. He was a good dancer, and Presley imagined they were the couple in the yellow Christmas village house she loved.

Contentment flowed through her as they swayed to the soft music. She could stay in his arms forever and never get tired of it. She didn't want this moment to end. This felt real, but the proposal coming up was all part of the show.

As Michael Bublè sang the final few lines, Kade gazed at her with a tenderness that made her believe in the magic of Christmas love. "You're so beautiful," he said before covering her mouth with his, kissing her so sweetly as if savoring this moment too.

The song ended, and she expected the director to stop filming. Natasha motioned for them to keep going as Kade took both of Presley's hands in his. She was trembling but his grip was sure and solid as he said some sweet things about the first time he noticed her. This wasn't part of the script either, but Natasha kept the cameras rolling as Kade admitted how much he'd liked her but was afraid to say anything because she was his best friend's little sister.

Presley's head was spinning because he seemed sincere and like he really meant every word. "I tried not to fall in love with you," he said. "But I couldn't help it." He leaned down and kissed her softly. "You're irresistible, and I love you, Presley Windsor," he said when their lips parted. "And I need to ask you a question."

Kade dropped to one knee while Presley's mind replayed his words. Was he in love with her, or were those precious words all part of the act?

Shaking, she covered her mouth with her hand, trying to hide her emotions. Her thoughts raced as she watched him pull out a black velvet ring box from his pocket. Presley knew her mother's ring hadn't come in the ring box, so either Kade's mom had a spare one lying around, or the props master gave it to him.

"Stop," a shrill voice said just as Kade was about to open the ring box. His face darkened like a thundercloud as the room erupted into utter chaos. Presley turned to see one of the sound guys trying to get Jillian to leave the room, but she wouldn't budge. The curse words flying around the room would give the show an R rating as Natasha demanded to know who let Jillian in.

"Jillian," Kade said. "That's enough. You need to leave."

"No, Kade," Jillian said, holding her phone up as if she was recording this moment for her posterity. "I'm not going anywhere until your family and the rest of the world knows the truth."

"Jillian, what are you doing?" Marilyn asked, coming into the overcrowded room with the rest of Kade's family right behind her.

"I'm exposing Presley as a fraud and the publicity scheme she and her press agent came up with that involves Kade pretending to be her fiancé."

A buzzing sound filled Presley's head, and her vision blurred when she saw Jillian held a cell phone in her other hand. Presley recognized the case and knew it belonged to her. A few months ago, she'd disabled the passcode so she didn't have to bother with it when working out. She'd never worried about it because she always had her phone with her, but Natasha had forbidden any cell phones during filming and told her to leave it in her room.

"Kade, is that true?" his mother asked after Jillian read a text message from Brynlee that talked about their fake engagement and asked if she thought any of Kade's family knew the truth.

Before Kade answered, Jillian read another message from Zuri, where she asked Presley if she'd found someone to be her fiancé.

"It's not like what Jillian is saying," Kade said. "We didn't do this as a publicity stunt."

"Then why did you do it?" his mother asked. Marilyn looked at Presley, disappointment reflected in her eyes. "Was this some kind of game to you?"

Every part of Presley's body was shaking so much that she wasn't sure how she was still standing. She licked her lips, trying to get enough moisture back in her mouth so she could talk. "No," she choked out. "This started out as a misunderstanding." Her voice was raw and came out barely above a whisper. "We didn't mean to hurt anyone."

"Well, you did," Marilyn said. "You came here, inserting yourself into our family and winning over the love of my grandchildren." Marilyn put an arm around Stacie's shoulders. "Making my daughters think they were gaining a sister when you never had any intention of marrying my son."

That's where she was wrong. Presley wanted to marry Kade, but getting married required both parties felt the same way. Kade wasn't ready for marriage, and the sad truth was that he might never want to get married.

A sob broke through as Presley looked at each of Kade's sisters. Each one stared at her as if she was some kind of monster. Like they were horrified they'd ever let her interact with their children.

"Mother!" Kade called out. "This is not Presley's fault."

"So you came up with this plan?" Jillian asked. She held out Presley's phone with the picture of her trying on rings with her brother. "This isn't you, Kade. This is Presley's older brother."

"Is that true?" Ben asked since Marilyn was now crying.

"Yes," Kade answered, rubbing a hand across his jaw. "I can

explain everything." Then he narrowed his eyes at Jillian. "Are you live streaming this?" he asked.

"People deserve the truth," Jillian said, not denying the accusation.

Natasha was furious all over again, threatening all kinds of lawsuits. None of it phased Jillian. She continued to record the events as if she was doing something noble and saving the world.

Presley couldn't take it anymore. She needed to leave but had no idea what to do since Jillian still had her phone. She could hear some of the kids crying, which broke her heart even more. Slipping behind one of the camera guys, Presley left the room and hurried up the stairs. No one came after her except for Lilly.

"Ah, honey, don't cry," Lilly said, wrapping her thin arms around Presley and hugging her. Presley gave into the hug, needing someone on her side. "It's going to be okay," Lilly soothed.

No, it wasn't going to be okay. Nobody could fix this—not even her big brother. Still, Presley needed Travis and Brynlee. They were the only family she had. The only family she might ever have.

"Lilly, is there any chance I can get a ride out of here?" Presley asked as she stepped back to wipe her face.

"Sure, but I'm going back to LA."

"That's okay, I just need to find a rental car and will have a better chance in LA."

"Oh, then we can stop at the rental car place on the way out of town. One of the guys is staying in Big Bear for Christmas to go skiing, and he rented a car when we first got in this morning."

"That's perfect." Presley didn't take time to change out of her dress. She shoved all of her clothes into her suitcase and then grabbed the small duffle that had all her toiletries in it and followed Lilly down the stairs.

There was still a lot of angry voices coming from the living room as she and Lilly exited through the front door. Pausing at the threshold, Presley looked at the beautiful house one last time. She blinked against the burning behind her eyes as despair pooled in her stomach, and she pulled the door closed, silencing the voices and leaving her broken heart behind.

CHAPTER 18

KADE

Kade had only felt this much anger a few times in his life, usually at work if he was called on a scene where innocent children were hurt. He still couldn't believe Jillian was doing this to him. To his family. To Presley.

Knowing he needed to go to her, he glanced to his right and found the place where she'd stood was empty. His gut twisted with renewed anxiety as he searched the room, looking for her. Where was she?

Jillian was still recording this entire mess. In three long strides, he reached out and snatched the phone from her.

"Excuse me!" she said, trying to grab it back.

"Give me Presley's phone," he said, holding Jillian's out of reach. He wanted to turn around and hurl her phone into the fireplace but needed it as leverage.

Outrage filled Jillian's face. "Give me my phone first."

"You know this is still recording you, right?" he asked.

She immediately changed her demeanor, so she didn't look like a raging lunatic. "Please return my phone," she said, handing over Presley's.

Kade ended the recording before handing it back to her. "Get out," he said, barely refraining from using a few words he'd picked up at the fire department.

"I'm a guest of your mother," she said, slipping her cell phone down into a hidden pocket of the gold dress she was wearing.

"Not anymore," Stacie said, coming to stand by Kade. "Way to ruin Christmas and your relationship with this family."

Jillian's face paled as if she'd expected everyone to start cheering and hugging her for exposing and eliminating the threat to the family. "I only wanted to tell the truth."

"Oh, so you figured live streaming it on social media was the way to do it?" Stacie seethed. His sister looked like she was mad enough to cause bodily harm to Jillian. "What you did was selfish and vicious." Stacie's voice broke as tears filled her eyes. Her hormones were yo-yo-ing all over the place. "You are a terrible person, and I would say more but my daughter is watching," Stacie said, breaking down and crying.

"Come here, sweetie," Greg said, putting his arm around his wife's shoulders. "Let's get Maddie and take her downstairs."

Jillian looked hollowed out as she looked around her. It looked like a war zone with kids crying, the production crew packing up, and the director on the phone, still yelling obscenities Kade didn't want any of his nieces and nephews to ever repeat. "Where's Marilyn?" Jillian asked in a small voice.

"She's in her room," Jamie said, trying to soothe little Blake. "Please don't go and talk to her. You broke Mom's heart tonight, Jillian. You broke a lot of hearts."

Presley's phone buzzed in his hand, reminding him that she wasn't here. He glanced down and saw it was a text from Zuri, telling her to call back immediately. "I need to find Presley," Kade said, trying to squeeze between Jillian and one of the sound guys.

"Kade," Jillian said, grabbing onto his arm. "I…I'm sorry."

Christmas was the season of giving, but Kade didn't know if he could ever give this woman his forgiveness. Still, he knew what holding onto a grudge did to a person. It had taken years to move past what his father had done to him when he was little. He still carried a lot of baggage, but he'd let go of the anger.

"I'm going to need a lot of time, Jillian." He pulled his arm from her grasp. "Despite how this all started, I'm in love with Presley and want to marry her." He felt for the ring box in his pocket and was relieved it was still there. It was kind of a blur after Jillian hijacked the proposal.

Tears mixed with mascara streamed down Jillian's face, making her look like a specter from a horror film. She didn't try to stop Kade this time as he slipped past her and took the stairs two at a time.

"Presley," Kade said, knocking on the closed bedroom door. He didn't wait for her to answer and twisted the knob, swinging the door open to an empty room. "Presley," he called again, rushing across the floor to knock on the bathroom door.

After discovering the bathroom was empty, Kade checked the closet and saw she'd cleared out her clothing. She'd left him.

Not that he blamed her.

Sitting on the edge of the bed, he pulled at the tie and unbuttoned the top button of his shirt, not sure what to do next.

"You're going after her, right?" Stacie said from the doorway.

Kade looked up and saw Allie and Jamie standing beside Stacie, both of them asking the same thing.

"Yes, but I'm not sure where she is or who she got a ride with." He held up her cell. "She left her phone behind."

"Call her brother," all three of his sisters said in unison.

That was one phone call Kade did not look forward to, but it was all he had since he was pretty sure Presley wasn't hiding somewhere in the house. Pulling his cell from the inside pocket of his suit coat, he tapped on the screen and pressed the call icon next to Travis's name. "Can you give me a minute?" he asked his sisters as the call went through.

"Sure," Jamie said.

"We want details," Stacie added.

Allie smiled and gave him the thumbs up. "Good luck."

"Dude, so how's it going?" Travis asked, clearly oblivious to what was going down. "Presley texted Brynlee last night and said she needed radio silence so she could follow through with her plan."

"Yeah, so that text wasn't from Presley."

The conversation went surprisingly well, considering Travis only threatened to kill Kade a few times. At least by the time

Kade got to the part that he was in love with his little sister and wanted to marry her, Brynlee had received a text from an unknown phone number from Presley that said she was renting a car and would be in Oceanside in a few hours.

"So you're really in love with my baby sister?" Travis asked.

"Yes." Kade ran a hand through his messy hair. The stylist had put some kind of product in it, making his hair hard to smooth down. "I love her." He let out a shaky laugh. "I know it sounds crazy, but I love her and want to marry her."

"What is it you're always telling me?" Travis asked, humor lacing the tone of his voice. "That love has made me stupid?"

"I was wrong," Kade said. "You're only stupid if you fall in love and don't do anything about it."

"So what are you going to do about it?" Travis asked.

"I have no idea." He glanced at the doorway. "But I have three sisters eavesdropping right now that will help me come up with a plan."

Stacie poked her head in the door. "Now we're talking," she said, coming into the room with Jamie and Allie right behind her.

Before Kade hung up, Travis promised to text when Presley arrived at Brynlee's parents' house. "Hey," Travis added. "I couldn't have picked a better man for my sister."

"Thanks, man," Kade said, feeling all choked up. "I just hope she'll want me too."

Kade ended the call and dropped the phone onto the bed. "I think I have an idea," he said, as a plan formed in his mind.

CHAPTER 19

PRESLEY

Christmas morning came way too early. Presley pulled the covers over her head, feeling like Scrooge and the Grinch rolled into one. "What time is it?" she said when Brynlee bounced on the bed.

"Time to get up." Brynlee pulled at the covers and grinned. "Hurry, Santa came, and I can't wait to see what he brought."

Presley's eyes felt gritty. Crying for three hours straight did that to a girl. "I need at least ten minutes with my makeup, so I don't scare your parents."

"You don't look that bad." Brynlee tipped her head to the side and squinted. "Okay, so I've seen you look better."

"Ha," Presley said, throwing a pillow at her. "I need you to be nice to me."

"Wait right there," Brynlee said, getting off the bed. "I need to get something from my room."

"I'm not going anywhere," Presley said, laying back down to stare at the ceiling. Part of her wondered if everything that had happened yesterday was all just a really bad nightmare. But then she remembered watching Jillian's video last night. It had gone viral and was trending more than parents tracking where Santa's sleigh was.

After arriving in Oceanside, Presley had purchased a burner phone at a convenience store and called her brother for the Taylor's address. Clearly, Travis had talked with Kade. He said Kade was worried about her and encouraged her to call him. Presley couldn't bring herself to make the call. She'd already ruined Christmas Eve day. No need to ruin his night too.

Travis, Brynlee, and Presley had all watched the video together, and it was as bad as she remembered. The worst part was what Marilyn had said to her. Kade's family would never forgive her, and she didn't blame them.

"No more crying," Brynlee said, coming back into the guest room Presley was staying in. "Someone gave this to me after I broke up with my college boyfriend, and it was just what I needed."

"A bottle of Jack Daniel's," Presley said, even though neither she or Brynlee drank.

"Ha ha." Brynlee pulled the covers back. "Sit up so I can show you."

Presley sat up and saw Brynlee clutching a wooden sign to her chest. "I met Travis a few months later, so I know it's true."

She turned the sign around and let Presley read it out loud. "Not to spoil the ending, but it will all be okay."

"It *is* going to be okay," Brynlee said. "I promise you."

"But what if Kade doesn't want to date me anymore?" Presley was pretty sure she'd cried all the tears out, but her eyes filled with moisture. "Even if he does, I doubt his family will ever speak to me again. You should've seen the looks on their faces."

"Don't you think their reaction had more to do with Jillian than you?" Brynlee asked.

"Not his mom." Presley squeezed her eyes shut. "I mean, she was barely tolerating me before Jillian exposed me as a liar and a fake."

"It will be okay," Brynlee said again. "Go wash your face and put on a little makeup." She winked at Presley. "I have it on good authority that Santa left you a few presents under the tree too."

"They better not be presents you were supposed to get," Presley said.

"Nope, they are definitely not mine." She patted Presley's leg. "Come on, it's Christmas morning and…"

"It will all be okay," Presley said, wishing she could believe that.

It took her fifteen minutes to put on her makeup, so she didn't look like she had dark circles under her eyes. Mr. and Mrs. Taylor greeted her with a cup of hot cocoa and a cheerful Merry Christmas when Presley arrived in the living room.

Brynlee was sitting on Travis's lap, both of them wearing matching Santa hats. "Merry Christmas," Presley said. She smiled and took a seat on the chair next to Travis and Brynlee. She was determined not to ruin anyone else's Christmas.

As Mr. Taylor distributed the gifts from under the tree, Presley imagined what Christmas morning was like at Kade's cabin. She wished she could be there to see Maddie and Brooklyn get matching dollhouses with all the accessories a little girl could ever want. Jenny and Laura were getting American Girl dolls that had been specially ordered to look like them. Jamie even had matching dresses for the girls to wear with their dolls. Lucas was getting a new Star Wars Legos set that Cody might be just as excited to play with.

"Presley, it's your turn," Brynlee said.

Presley blinked and realized everyone was waiting for her to open her gift. "Sorry," she said, glancing down at the package. There was a tag addressed to Presley from Tiny Tad. "Who's Tiny Tad?"

"Santa's special elf," Brynlee answered. "It says it in the fine print."

"Thanks, Tiny Tad," Presley said, rereading the name tag, this time seeing the small writing along the bottom of the paper. She ripped the paper and opened the box to find a gingerbread house kit. Tears stung her eyes as she pulled it from the box. Tiny Tad had no way of knowing that this would remind her of Kade's family tradition. "This is awesome," she said, glancing at Mrs. Taylor. She was likely Tiny Tad. "Thank you."

"Don't thank, Mom," Brynlee said. "Tiny Tad brought it."

"Right," Presley said, unable to hold back a laugh. She loved Brynlee and couldn't wait until Travis married her.

Another round of gifts was opened with Presley going last again. Not surprisingly, this gift was from Santa's elf too. Peeling off the wrapping paper, she opened the lid of the box to find a Christmas ornament made from glass with the words *It's Not Easy Being a Princess* etched into it. "Ah, this is so sweet," she said, holding up the ornament. "Where did you find it?"

"Tiny Tad, remember?" Brynlee said.

"I love it." She placed the ornament back into the box and accepted another gift from Mr. Taylor.

Brynlee opened two gifts since she had the most under the tree. Presley was last again. Prying the lid from the box, she almost stopped breathing as she stared at the gift. It was the yellow Christmas village house with the dancing couple in the window. "How did you get this?" Her voice sounded thick, and she gently cleared her throat. "And don't tell me it's from Tiny Tad."

"But it is from Tiny Tad," a man's voice said from behind her. "He's been coming to our family for several generations."

A flood of emotions ripped through Presley like a tornado and hurricane making landfall at the same time. She turned and saw Kade standing there, dressed in a pair of Christmas PJ's that made him look both sexy and adorable. She wanted to run into his arms but decided to wait and see exactly why he was here.

"You came after me?" she asked, unable to wait another moment for an explanation.

"Yeah," Kade said, looking a little unsure of himself. "I got here last night and slept in the Taylor's guest house."

"Kade, but what about your family?"

Giving her a censuring look, he came around and held out his hand. "You left me last night." She placed her palm against his, and he tugged a little to help her stand up. "Don't ever leave me again," he said before wrapping his arms around her and kissing her thoroughly. Presley melted like chocolate too close to the fire as Kade worked Christmas magic with his mouth, making her not care that her brother was watching his best friend kiss his sister.

"I love you," Kade whispered against her lips.

Gasping, she leaned back to catch her breath and looked into his smoldering eyes. "What did you just say?"

Grinning, Kade pressed a light kiss to her lips. "I love you, Presley." He kissed her again. "I love you and want to spend forever with you."

Presley was too stunned to speak. Heck, she could hardly breathe.

"Psst," Brynlee said. "This is where you tell him you love him too."

"I love you too." She bit down on her bottom lip. "But what about your family?"

"My family adores you."

Unable to believe him, she dropped her chin and pressed her forehead into his chest. "How can they after I lied to them about us being engaged?"

Kade's soft laughter rumbled in his chest. "Presley, you didn't lie to them."

She tipped her face up and narrowed her eyes. "Um, yeah, it's all over the internet."

"Jillian's version is all over the internet." Kade let go of her and produced the black ring box, holding it out in front of him. "I was about to make an honest woman out of you when Jillian crashed the scene."

Kade dropped to one knee, making Presley draw in another sharp breath. "Kade," she said, covering her mouth with her hand. "What are you doing?" she asked through her shaking fingers.

"Presley Windsor, I love you more than I ever thought was possible, and I promise to love you every day that we have together. Please make this the best Christmas ever and say that you'll marry me?"

Presley tried not to cry. She didn't want to mess up her makeup again, but the tears came anyway. Especially when Kade opened the lid to reveal the most gorgeous ring she'd ever seen. "Is this Grandma Hunter's ring?" she asked, staring at the platinum setting with a large diamond surrounded by smaller diamonds.

"It's your ring now, but only if you say yes."

"Yes," she said with a breathless laugh. "I said yes, didn't' I?"

"You did now," Travis said. He and Brynlee were standing close, both of them smiling. "Let the guy put the ring on your finger already."

Kade took the ring out and took hold of Presley's left hand. She could feel Kade trembling as much as she was. He poised it at the tip of her finger and paused. "If it doesn't fit, then we'll get it sized."

"Okay." He started to slide it on, but Presley stopped him. "Wait, I'm serious about your family. Your mother must hate me."

"Do you trust me?" Kade asked in a serious voice.

"Yes," Presley said, nodding her head.

Without saying another word, Kade slid the beautiful ring onto her finger. It was a little snug but not too uncomfortable. His eyes traced her face as he stood up and lifted her left hand to his mouth, pressing his lips to her knuckles.

Brynlee squealed and moved in for a hug. "Congratulations!" she said, squeezing all the air out of Presley's lungs. "I'm so happy for you."

Travis was next, picking her up and hugging her tightly. "I'm so happy for you," he said, his voice thick with emotion. Then he turned to Kade and gave him a quick, hard hug. "So does this mean you're my little brother now?" he teased.

"I'm older than you and taller by an inch, so no," Kade said, slugging him playfully in the arm.

Mr. and Mrs. Taylor congratulated both of them, welcoming Kade to the family.

Presley held out her left hand, letting the diamond catch the light. "It's so beautiful," she said, rising on her toes to kiss Kade. "Thank you," she murmured against his lips. "You are the best Christmas surprise I'll ever get."

"I have one more surprise," Kade said, taking her by the hand and leading her toward the front door. "Close your eyes." He let go of her hand. "And no peeking until I tell you."

Presley squeezed her eyes shut and felt the cool morning air drift over her when he opened the door. "Can I look yet?" Presley asked, pretty sure she heard voices that sounded like kids.

"You can look," Kade said, threading his fingers through hers and pulling her outside.

"Merry Christmas!" Kade's family shouted when Presley opened her eyes. She blinked a few times to clear her vision, but Kade's entire family was still there, all of them wearing the exact same Christmas pajamas as Kade had on.

"Did she say yes?" Stacie called out, her baby bump looking so cute in the thermal type pajama top and matching flannel bottoms.

Presley held up her left hand. "I said yes!" she said, still unable to believe Kade's family had driven all the way to Oceanside on Christmas morning.

The group converged on her, the children reaching her first. Presley finally understood the meaning of the Grinch's heart growing three sizes as she hugged every single child, loving their little arms around her. Next, Cody, Devon, and Greg hugged her, welcoming her to the family. Kade's sisters were next. It was more like a big group hug as they thanked her for giving their brother a second chance.

The last two people to approach her were Kade's mom and stepdad. "Welcome to the family, sweetheart," Ben said, hugging her. "You're good for our family, and we look forward to many more Christmases with you and Kade."

Presley gave him an extra hug before facing Kade's mom. Marilyn looked like she'd been crying. Was that because she didn't want to be here? "I'm so sorry," Presley said.

Marilyn shook her head. "You have nothing to apologize for." Her eyes shimmered with tears as she reached out and took Presley's hands in hers. "I'm the one who needs to apologize." She glanced at Kade. "To both of you. I was blinded by what I thought was best." She gave Kade a warm smile. "I'm so proud of the man you are, Kade, and I'm sorry for not telling you that sooner."

"Thanks, Mom," Kade said, his voice cracking with emotion.

Marilyn looked at Presley. "I truly am sorry," she said, squeezing Presley's fingers. "And I hope you can forgive me."

"I already have," Presley said. "I love your son, and I promise I'll keep him in line for you."

"Hey," Kade said as his siblings doubled over in laughter. "I'm not that bad."

While Presley enjoyed making the others laugh, it was the radiant smile on Marilyn's face that filled her with joy, making her body feel as light as a balloon filled with helium. "You, darling girl, are his perfect match."

"Thank you, Marilyn." Presley blinked rapidly so she didn't start bawling again. "That means a lot to me."

Marilyn held out her arms, and Presley stepped into the hug, inhaling Marilyn's expensive perfume. "I don't want you to call me Marilyn," Kade's mom said, pulling back but keeping her hands on Presley's shoulders. "I want you to call me Mom."

"Mom," Presley repeated. "I love that name, and I haven't used it for a very long time."

Now Marilyn was the one blinking rapidly. "Don't make me cry," she said, waving her hand in front of her face.

"Grammy," Jenny and Laura said in unison. "Can we give Aunt Presley her present now?'

"Oh my gosh," Presley said, leaning into Kade's side. "They just called me Aunt Presley."

He laughed and pressed a kiss on the top of her head as the girls handed Presley a gift wrapped box. "Is this one from Tiny Tad too?" Presley asked, looking for a name tag.

"No, it's from all of us," Marilyn said.

Presley had the twins help her rip away the paper. Lifting the lid, she stared at the final gift as if she'd just received a check for a million dollars. "These are for me?" she asked, hugging the box to her chest. "I have to go put them on."

Feeling like she couldn't be any happier, Presley raced into the guest bedroom and stripped out of her clothes. Without taking the tags off, she donned the matching Christmas pajamas Kade and his family had on.

"Ta da," she said, striking a pose on the front porch.

While the family cheered, Kade snagged her around the waist and gave her a quick peck. "I'm not done kissing you," he said, taking her hand and leading her off of the front porch. "But first, it's family picture time."

Brynlee was into photography and had taken some online classes after Travis gave her a high-end digital camera for her birthday last month. With Travis's help, she ordered Kade's family where to stand. They were grouped in families with Marilyn and Ben standing in the center. "Let's have Kade and Presley stand in the middle too," Brynlee said when she and Kade didn't know where to stand.

The only time Presley had ever been in a group photo this big was when she was in grade school, and it was class picture day. Brynlee took several pictures of them all smiling. The kids started getting restless, so she had them all make funny faces.

"One more," Greg said, who was just behind Presley and Kade. "With mistletoe hanging above the newly engaged couple." He dangled a familiar sprig of green over their heads.

"We have to kiss," Presley said, tipping her face up to Kade. "It's tradition."

"And a fun one at that," Kade said, lowering his head to meet her lips in a kiss filled with Christmas magic and the promise to love her forever.

EPILOGUE

Presley closed her eyes while Lilly finished her makeup for the live interview. "I wish you could move into my house and do my makeup every day," Presley said, opening her eyes when Lilly finished applying the mascara. "You always make me look so good."

"It's not hard to do with a face like yours." Lilly held up the finishing spray, waiting until Presley closed her eyes again before spritzing a fine mist to seal the makeup. "And you're a newlywed, so I don't think your husband would like me moving in with you."

Her husband. Presley still couldn't believe she was married to Kade Hunter. She opened one eye and peeked at the diamond ring on her left hand. Grandma Hunter's ring was even more beautiful, paired with the wedding band Kade had slipped on her finger when they'd married three weeks after Christmas.

"Perfect," Lilly said, taking off the white apron protecting Presley's black cocktail dress. "You look stunning."

"She does," Kade said, leaning against the doorjamb and looking at Presley with his smoldering blue eyes. She knew that look well. But whatever plans he had in mind would have to wait. They were going live in ten minutes. "And, no, Lilly can't move in with us," he said with a smirk.

"Do not mess up her hair or makeup," Lilly said as Kade sauntered over to get Presley. "You can ravish your wife once the interview is over."

"Seriously?" Kade said, taking Presley's hand to help her stand up. "Not even one kiss?"

"Not even one," Lilly said.

"Hello, handsome husband," Presley said, wishing she could sneak off with him for a mini make out session. But Lilly was watching them like a hawk. On more than one occasion, she'd had to fix Presley's makeup because of Kade.

"Hi, beautiful wife." He pressed a kiss to the top of her head.

"I saw that," Lilly said. "Let's get you on the set before you're tempted to break the rules."

"You know how I feel about rules," Kade said under his breath.

"Yes, you don't like to follow them." Presley laughed and leaned into his side as they followed Lilly down the narrow hallway. "I see you declined to wear a tie," Presley said, glancing over at Kade. He looked pretty good wearing dark dress pants and a white dress shirt tailored to fit him perfectly.

"Ties feel like they're choking me."

"I didn't say I didn't like it." She winked at him. "You look very sexy, and I'm glad I get to take you home after."

"Can't we just leave now?" Kade asked as they approached the end of the hall. "Zuri already posted wedding pics."

"This is the last interview," Presley said. "Zuri promised."

"I still can't believe you hired her full-time."

"If it weren't for her, we wouldn't be together." Besides, Zuri wasn't acting as Presley's agent. Presley had signed with one of the top agents right before she married Kade. Zuri was strictly in charge of the Princess Warrior's online presence and social media accounts. But this interview had been in the works before the wedding so Zuri was taking credit for it.

Kade took her hand and threaded their fingers together. "I guess that's probably fair to say."

It was true. Kade had admitted that he probably would have never dared ask Presley out. The whole fake fiancé thing had turned out to be the best thing to ever happen to both of them.

After Jillian's video went viral, followers had done the opposite of what Jillian had hoped to accomplish. They loved that Kade had posed as her fiancé and then fallen in love with her.

The hype only escalated from there when Brynlee posted the video of Kade proposing to Presley on Christmas morning. It got two million more views than Jillian's in the first twenty-four hours. Presley and Kade had become celebrities and had made the rounds to different morning shows across the nation.

This was their first post-wedding interview that the network had exclusive rights to air. Presley and Kade were leaving for their long-overdue honeymoon as soon as they were done here. They'd delayed going for three months since filming for *American Ninja Champions* was started a few weeks after they got married.

As much as she hated being away from Kade, Presley had spent every moment training for the upcoming season. At least the actual filming only took seven days, so she and Kade got to spend more time acting like newlyweds.

She and the other contestants were under a strict gag order to not discuss the outcome. It wasn't until a few nights ago that the finale of *American Ninja Champions* aired. The Princess Warrior had made it all the way to the final episode, coming in second to veteran Melanie Andrews, also known as Mighty Mel, making a comeback after sitting out the last two seasons to have a baby. Poison Ivy was eliminated during the third tier and made a vow to Melanie and Presley to watch out because she was coming back next year.

Presley knew a rematch with Ivy wasn't going to happen next season. Actually, no one other than Presley, her agent, and the morning show host knew she wouldn't be competing next year either. Kade would know soon enough, and she hoped he would be as happy as she was.

"Please come this way," an assistant to the producer said as she led them to the set and introduced them to the morning show host, Hellen Dymock. Presley had met her earlier but was supposed to act like this was the first time.

"It's a pleasure to meet you," Hellen said, air-kissing Presley.

"Thank you," Presley said, taking a seat on an off-white leather loveseat. Kade started to sit next to her but stopped when Hellen grabbed his hand.

"We're excited to have you here too," she said, leaning in to give him an air kiss.

"Thank you, ma'am," Kade said. "I'm excited to be here too."

Presley knew Kade really wasn't excited to be here but did it because he loved her. She'd also promised him a back rub later on tonight if he did this one last interview.

Hellen still held Kade's hand as she addressed the live audience. "Didn't y'all just melt when this man proposed to Presley on Christmas morning?"

Color infused Kade's face as the women in the audience started whistling and clapping for him. Looking mildly uncomfortable from all the attention, Presley was glad when Hellen let go of Kade's hand and indicated for him to sit down.

Settling close to her, Kade slid his arm across Presley's shoulders. "You so owe me that back rub," he whispered when he leaned in and pressed a kiss to the side of her head.

"Hmm-mm," she said, knowing that by the end of the day, Kade would be pampering her like she really was a princess.

The producer gave the cue, and Hellen introduced Presley and Kade for the viewers at home, giving them a brief synopsis of how their relationship started and then talked about them falling in love while pretending to be engaged. They touched briefly on the rocky Christmas Eve but didn't show any clips from Jillian's video.

Presley and Kade made the stipulation that no part of Jillian's video could be aired. It was a difficult situation because of the family's long-time friendship. Kade and Presley had chosen to forgive Jillian for his parent's sake but knew it would never be the same. At least Jillian had moved on. Literally. She'd taken a job in London and seemed to be happy.

The live audience loved seeing clips from the video of Kade proposing Christmas morning. They also loved the picture of the whole family dressed in matching Christmas pajamas.

Hellen asked about the wedding and was thrilled to share exclusive wedding photographs with the audience. Presley and Kade answered her questions about the marriage, knowing the host wanted to talk about the outcome of the *American Ninja Champion's* final show.

"How are you feeling about coming in second?" Hellen asked Presley.

"I feel awesome," Presley answered. "I was so happy for Melanie. She's amazing and has worked hard getting in shape after having her baby."

"That was quite the comeback," Hellen said. "I know fans are happy to see her since she wasn't sure she would keep competing once she and her husband started their family." Hellen smiled at the audience before turning to look at Presley. "I have to ask since Poison Ivy has indicated she is excited about a rematch. Does this mean fans will see the Princess Warrior for the following *American Ninja Champion* season?"

That was Presley's cue. Her stomach twisted with nerves, making her wish there was a trashcan nearby. She'd been queasy the past two weeks but didn't ever throw up. She sure hoped that trend continued.

"I'm glad you asked, Hellen," Presley said. "But the answer is no. I will not be returning for the next season." Presley had one hand on Kade's knee and felt him stiffen. She gently squeezed his leg and turned to look at him. "For the next nine months, I'll be training for something I've never done before."

Kade's eyes widened with surprise. This was all news to him. "What are you talking about?" he asked, licking his lips. "I thought you wanted to give next year another shot?"

"I did, but our plans have changed." Presley couldn't hold it in any longer. She turned back to Hellen, who was holding a gift bag out to her. "This is for you," she said, taking the bag and handing it to Kade.

"What's this for?" he asked, moving his arm from around her so he could use both hands to open the gift bag.

"Open it and see," she said, glancing out to the live audience. Travis and Brynlee were there along with Kade's parents, his sisters, and their husbands.

Kade's hands were trembling as he pulled the tissue paper out of the bag. He hesitated for just a moment, meeting Presley's gaze briefly before pulling out a small t-shirt made for a baby. "Oh wow," he said, his voice catching as he held out the shirt in front of him that said, 'Baby Hunter...coming next Christmas.'

"Surprise!" Presley said with a small laugh.

"I'm going to be a dad?" Kade asked. "For real?"

"Yes," Presley said over the audience, clapping and whistling. "For real."

"Yes!" Kade said, pumping his fist in the air. He jumped up and swept Presley into his arms, spinning her around once before putting her on her feet. "I love you so much."

"I love you too," she said breathlessly. "So you're happy?" she whispered, blinking back the moisture filling her eyes.

"So happy," Kade said. He lowered his mouth to hers and said in a low voice, "I'm not sure what the network rules are, but I'm going to kiss you right now, and it will probably mess up your hair and makeup."

"It's about time," Presley said. "Besides, the rules are more like guidelines, love," she murmured before pulling his mouth to hers.

Kade kissed her long and slow, tunneling his fingers into her hair and doing a thorough job of messing up her perfect curls. With a sigh of pure happiness, Presley melted in her husband's arms, relishing in the feel of his lips. The Princess Warrior had found her Prince Charming, and she knew they were going to live happily ever after.

Thank you so much for reading *Her Stand-in Fake Fiancé*! I hope you enjoyed reading Presley and Kade's story as much as I loved writing it.

Please consider leaving a review. (Pretty please! Reviews are so important to an author and to other readers!) Besides all of that, I truly appreciate every single one!

FREE BOOK

Thank you so much for reading *Her Stand-in Fake Fiancé*. If you liked it, I hope you'll consider leaving a review for it on Amazon and GoodReads. If you'd like to receive updates on my books, as well as notices about new releases and sales on books from authors like me, please sign up for my Newsletter and receive a FREE copy of *The Cowboy's Accidental Bride* just for signing up.

Thank you again for reading my books! My readers are the best and make writing worth it.

All the best,
Cindy

ABOUT THE AUTHOR

Cindy Roland Anderson is an Amazon best-selling author who writes clean, contemporary romance with a combination of humor, romantic tension and some pretty great kissing scenes. She and her husband live in northern Utah, and are parents to five children, and grandparents to eight adorable grandchildren. She is a registered nurse and has worked in the NICU as well as the newborn nursery. She loves to read, almost as much as she loves writing. And she loves chocolate... probably a little too much.

Be sure and sign up for Cindy's Newsletter and receive a free copy of one of her books. You'll also get notified first of her latest book release and the chance to receive an advanced copy of that new book before anyone else.

To see all her works please visit Cindy Roland Anderson's Author Page

Cindy loves to hear from her readers! To notify her please visit her website http://www.cindyrolandanderson.com

The Rogue Warrior

Individual Titles

Fair Catch

Discovering Sophie

The Cowboy's Accidental Bride

Second Chance Kisses

Made in the USA
Monee, IL
10 July 2022

99443709R00125